THE SCORE KEEPER

BOSTON HAWKS HOCKEY
BOOK 9

GINA AZZI

THREE CITIES PUBLISHING LLC

PROLOGUE

SCOTT

I notice her the moment she enters the space; I always do.

Sure, the gala is beautiful. The venue, unparalleled. The menu has been prepared by a world-renowned chef and the cocktails created by mixologists from the city's top bars. With the city bustling around us—Manhattan in summertime—it's like no other place in the world.

And the woman is like no other woman.

She's breathtakingly stunning, almost too gorgeous to look at. She's not standoffish, the way one would expect, but gives off a sincere, down-to-earth energy she must have inherited from her late mother. Her father, a giant among New York society, is gruff and demanding, argumentative.

As heiress to the New York Sharks franchise, one would think Noelle DiSanto would be the same. If I hadn't known her for years, hadn't observed her for the last several, I would think that. But on two different occasions, both over five years ago, Noelle and I shared more than our link to the hockey world. We shared drinks, deep conversation, and searing kisses that are still imprinted on my mind. Soon after, she started dating one of her father's top hockey players and I learned to keep my distance.

She approaches the bar, a wide smile on her face. Her gown, a deep gold that highlights her tan and offers a peek of her thighs with a delicious slit up the side, ripples as she moves. She leans over the bar and says something that causes the bartender to laugh and nod, to enjoy pouring her a glass of pinot noir when his night has probably been spent serving wealthy pricks with sticks up their asses.

She chats with the bartender effortlessly and accepts her wine. Flashing him a grin, she turns, her eyes scanning the expansive space. Is she looking for her date? A rumble moves through my chest at the thought. I didn't see her come in with a man, but the chances that Noelle is on her own, when she looks this sexy, when she exudes this much light, is slim.

Her blonde ringlets are pulled back, a few curls springing loose to frame her face. Her eyes, deep blue, are large and expressive. The gold sheath of her dress clings to her curves, showing off her toned physique. She's rocking sapphire studs that cost a small fortune but other than her earrings, there's nothing about her that gives off how wealthy she is. And I like that about her.

In a room filled with posturing men and showy women, Noelle DiSanto is a true treasure. She would be easy to lavish with gifts and affection, not because she demands them but because she's so damn worthy. Because she doesn't *need* the attention. I lift my old-fashioned to my mouth and take a sip, trying not to recall the night we indulged in bourbon, and I tasted the sweetness of her lips more than the cinnamon of the alcohol.

A man approaches her, and she gives a friendly smile but extricates herself from the conversation before it can really begin. I hide my chuckle in another sip of my drink.

As owner of the Boston Hawks Hockey team, I'm used to dating women who have high expectations. Women with desires of attaining a certain social standing. Women who like gifts more for the material item and less for the meaning behind it.

The refreshing thing about Noelle is that she's already acquired a lofty social status. She is well-known and connected throughout New York society. She's financially capable of taking care of herself. And every man in this room knows it.

Still, it doesn't stop their approaches, each one more desperate than the last to get in good with her father, a man who has significant pull in the best city in the country.

I finish my drink, knowing I need to stop checking out my biggest rival's daughter before he pummels me. I snort, the thought of Rick DiSanto getting in one punch comical when a friendly voice interrupts my thoughts.

"Scott, good to see you here," Mike Matero, Captain of the Sharks and one of my former players greets me.

I grin, holding out my hand and pulling Mike in for a hug. "Mikey, man, it's good to see you. Congrats on being named Captain," I say. Even though trading Mike was personally tough, it was best for the Hawks, and, turns out, best for his career. He wouldn't have been named Captain on my team because his brother-in-law, Austin Merrick, already holds that title and does a damn good job keeping it.

"Thanks, Scott. How are you?" Mike asks.

"Doing well. Eager for training camps to begin."

He chuckles. "Soon enough. You calling up Sims full-time?"

Inwardly, I groan. Eddie Sims cost us the play-offs when he was called in for Noah Scotch and couldn't get his shit together, playing hungover and having spent the night in jail after getting rounded up in a drug bust at an LA club. Sims caused us a publicity nightmare but he's still one of my guys, so I give a non-answer. "We'll see how training kicks off."

Mike grins, seeing straight through me.

I turn as a flash of gold moves in my peripheral vision and

watch as Rick approaches his daughter, a shmoozy douche at his side.

Mike follows my line of vision and groans. "Not Ben."

"Fucking Tully," I snarl. Ben Tully is one of Rick's inner circle, a VP in the Sharks franchise, and nowhere near good enough for Noelle.

"I swear, Rick tries to set his daughter up at every one of these events. We all know he's grooming her to take his place—"

I nod, because Rick's been shouting Noelle out for years.

"—but he wants her future husband to have a Sharks connection. Someone he can trust, someone he knows can lead beside her."

"Why not just trust her?" I ask, annoyed that Rick wants his daughter to succeed him but then doesn't trust her enough to do the job.

"Exactly," Mike agrees, surprising me. He turns away, muttering, "Each guy is worse than the last."

"Tully?" I question, wondering why he doesn't like the VP.

He taps the end of his nose, signaling a cocaine habit.

"Damn," I mutter, my annoyance morphing into anger. I glance at Noelle, note the tension in her expression, the tightness in her posture. No woman should have to put up with that shit but definitely not at the insistence of her father.

"There's Savannah." Mike indicates over my shoulder, spotting his wife. "Sorry, Scott, I better go. Vanny doesn't look good. I don't know why they call it morning sickness when it's all damn day."

"Go," I encourage him, grasping his shoulder. "And congrats on the baby, Mike. I'm happy for you and Vanny."

"Thanks. See you around." He takes off toward Savannah, and I turn my attention back to the beauty I can't stop checking out.

At the wayward expression on her face, I decide it's time to intervene.

Straightening my tie and squaring my shoulders, I head toward Noelle just as the band begins their next set.

As Rick and Ben talk hockey, clearly boring the hell out of Noelle, I cut in.

"Noelle DiSanto."

She looks up, her eyes flaring with a hint of desire as they drink me in. Does she remember our kiss as clearly as I do? She smiles warmly. "Scott Reland. I didn't expect to see you here."

"Why's that?"

"You hate these events," she reminds me.

I chuckle, tipping my head in agreement. I love hockey. I love the sport, I love the competitiveness, I love the team dynamic. But I hate all the schmoozy bullshit that comes with owning a team. The politics, the ass-kissing, the ridiculous events that encourage said ass-kissing. And five years ago, somewhere between wine and bourbon, I laid it all out for a tipsy Noelle.

"Rick, Ben," I say in greeting.

Ben says hello but Rick gives me a hard look and nods. Ah, that's as much as I'm going to get from him. We've been rivals for a long time, from before I was team owner. In fact, I inherited my rivalry with Rick, the same way he did. Boston and New York had a falling out years ago that led to players jumping ship, a questionable New York Cup win in the eighties, and a lasting dislike that continues until present day.

Still, he's my elder, has done right by Mike, and is the father of the woman I can't stop looking at, so I play it polite.

Holding out my hand, I ask Noelle, "Want to dance?"

She gives me an easy grin, relief sparking in her eyes. She places her hand in mine and I wrap my fingers around her smooth skin. "Sure."

I nod again to the men and lead Noelle to the dance floor.

Gathering her in my arms, we begin to dance, both of us relaxing as the gossip of the gala falls into the background.

"Thanks for the save," she says, confirming my hunch.

"You owe me one," I joke. For a second, her face falls and I worry my joke didn't land. I backpedal, "Didn't seem like Ben was doing it for you."

She groans but her expression turns playful. "Daddy wants what's best for me. But I don't know why he thinks that's finding a husband in the Sharks world."

I spin her, waiting until we're face-to-face to ask, "And what do you want?"

She rolls her lips together, thinking it over. "To grow my business," she says finally.

I frown. "The Sharks?"

"No," she says gently. "That's Dad's business. I opened a bakery."

"Here? In the city?" I'm impressed. Manhattan isn't an easy place to start a new business, especially when there are a multitude of bakeries on every street.

"Yes."

Slowly, pieces of information from long ago trickle through my mind. "That's right. You studied in France for a bit, didn't you?"

"You have a good memory, Scott."

"Hey, I'm not that old, Noelle," I feign offense.

She grins. "Forty-two?"

"You're sweet. Forty-four."

"Ah." Her palm slides higher up on my shoulder, her nails grazing gently. "I just celebrated thirty-four."

"Happy birthday," I tell her.

"Thank you. And yes, I studied at L'Ecole Lenôtre." She pronounces the French perfectly, hinting at her fluency in the language. "Although," she laughs, "my teacher, Madam Etienne, almost had a heart attack when she learned I'm specializing in cupcakes."

I laugh. "Scandalized by the bastardization of a good pastry by American consumerism."

"Extremely," Noelle agrees.

"And how's your bakery going?"

She beams, her eyes flashing. Lowering her voice, she whispers. "So good I'm scared to jinx it."

"Don't be. You put in the work, and starting your own business is a hell of a lot of work, so enjoy it when it's going well. Business is all ups and downs, oftentimes unexpected surprises."

"Yeah. But I love it."

"Me too. There's nothing like working for yourself."

"Exactly. I'm thinking about expanding, opening a new location. I've been on the Upper West Side for almost three years now."

"Considering downtown?"

She shakes her head. "No. I'm thinking a new city altogether. Maybe Philadelphia. Or D.C."

"Or Boston," I supply.

She smiles. "We'll see. Daddy's not completely on board. He wants me here for…all of this." Her eyes swing around the event space.

"Still wants you to take the reins?" I ask, even though I know the answer.

"Still expects it," she responds.

"Don't give up on what you want, Noelle," I advise, hating that I sound every bit my forty-four years compared to her thirty-four. But—"Business works best when your heart's in it."

"Thanks, Scotty."

I snort. "Scotty? No one's called me that in ages."

"Yeah, well, I've known you a long time."

"And I still wish you knew me better." I spin her again as the song comes to an end. "Don't be a stranger, Noelle."

She blushes, biting her bottom lip. "Thanks for the dance,

Scott," she says sweetly. "See you when the Sharks come to Boston?"

"Or when your bakery does."

She smiles and dips her head, pleased by my response.

I watch her walk back to her table, note the relaxed ease of her movements. The tension from earlier has dissipated and I'm happy I could help her enjoy a slice of tonight's event.

When she reaches the table, Rick turns and gives me a look. I ignore him because Noelle turns too. She gazes at me over her shoulder, her expression soft, her eyes searching.

I smile at her, my hands in my pockets, as I rock back on my heels.

She smiles back before her dad pulls her into a conversation. Immediately the tension in her shoulder returns, her spine straightening.

To everyone in this room, Noelle DiSanto is a lucky heiress. To me, she's a passionate woman with a wondrous heart and a generous soul.

She's the real sapphire.

CHAPTER 1
NOELLE

I take a cleansing exhale as I stand in front of my new bakery in downtown Boston. Primrose Sweets has expanded, and I've officially launched my second location. Pride fills me as I stare up at the beautiful signage, inspired by my mom's name, Rose Primeri. Primrose was Daddy's nickname for her. She passed when I was nine and I don't think he fully recovered from her loss. Chasing my dreams, learning the art of patisserie, and opening Primrose Sweets is my way of honoring the legacy she left behind: me.

I shiver against the winter chill and hurry back inside the warmth of the bakery. As soon as I open the door, the delicious scent of sugar and vanilla greets me, and I smile. The storefront is sweet and although the space is small, only holding nine tables, it's mine. Scott Reland was right, there's nothing like working for yourself.

Daddy thinks this is all a phase. He believes once I realize how hard it is to keep growing my bakeries, I'll come back to New York, begging for a job with the Sharks. While his lack of faith in my ability to be successful on my own hurts, I know it's partly driven by his own desire to keep the Sharks franchise in DiSanto hands.

Either way, this is my chance to prove myself. To him and to myself.

I tie an apron around my waist and move back behind the counter. Surveying the cupcakes and other baked goods I offer—croissants, eclairs, mille-feuille—I note that we've sold most of the sweets today. Relief spreads through my limbs, followed by a wave of satisfaction.

While I haven't let Dad's outlook stop me, his view has caused me to question if I can handle this. Can I really run two bakeries in two different cities? Can I keep turning a profit, growing, introducing new sweet-lovers to my desserts?

The task seems daunting and yet, as I glance around my tiny space in the heart of Boston, I can't remember the last time I was this happy. Well, I guess the day I opened my New York location. But that was three years ago and now, this feels like a big win. I've been in Boston for two weeks and from the first day our doors opened, I've experienced a steady trickle of business and a warm welcome to the city.

The mild success has softened the doubt Dad's words often cause. It's also helped ease the guilt I feel whenever I don't agree with Daddy, since Mom always did. I can still hear her voice gently reminding me to "obey your father," even when his rules seemed unfair.

I pour myself a fresh cup of coffee and watch as the first few snowflakes of the afternoon descend from the sky. It's not this cold in New York yet but winter is upon us. Dad argued this was a terrible time to open a bakery and while his reasoning made sense, when the lease for this space suddenly became available, I didn't question it.

I jumped in whole-heartedly and haven't looked back. The bell above the door chimes as a customer enters and I smile. Oftentimes, not looking back is the best thing I can do to keep moving forward.

The customer is carrying a vase with a beautiful floral arrangement.

"Would you like some sweet treats to go with your flower delivery?" I ask the young man who looks to be in his early twenties.

He shakes his head and places the vase down on the countertop. "These are for you." He frowns. "Well, maybe. Are you Noelle DiSanto?"

"I am."

"Then these are for you." He smirks, pushing the vase closer to my side of the counter.

"They are? Who sent them?"

He indicates the little notecard.

"Oh," I say surprised, wondering who sent me flowers. Maybe my Aunt Maria? Or my best friend from college, Tia? Or my New York manager and ride-or-die, Averie? Probably Averie.

The young man backs away and I spring into action.

"Here," I call out, opening the display case and placing an eclair in a bag. I hold it out to the guy.

"Hey, thanks."

"Tell your friends to come by," I encourage.

He nods and leaves the shop.

When I'm alone again, I pick up the card and trace the edge of the envelope flap. My heart rate increases as I think about who sent the flowers. For a brief instant, Scott Reland flickers through my mind.

At forty-four years old, he's sophisticated and confident. Tall, fit, and with the most alluring, bright green eyes, Scott's physical prowess almost rivals his sharp intelligence. He's quick, compassionate, and has the best sense of humor of anyone I've met in Daddy's hockey circles. While my father has disliked him for years, I've always enjoyed whenever our paths would cross. I bite my bottom lip recalling one night when our polite conversation turned to witty banter. Wine gave way to bourbon and longing gazes morphed into passionate kissing. Scott made me feel alive—*wanted*—and I couldn't get enough.

But the following day, as Dad berated his rival, I couldn't help but wonder if Scott kissed me because of the forbidden nature of such a hookup. It was the second time we kissed, and the fact that he never tried to take it further both confused and soothed me.

Soon after, I met Chris, and my kisses with Scott became fond memories of time spent with a long-held crush. I shake my head at the old memories.

But the last time I saw him, over the summer, the way he held me in his arms and spun me around the dance floor was different. Our public relationship, usually cordial with an easy affability, shifted into something more. The urgency of our kisses from so long ago seemed present again. There was a charge I hadn't detected in years. I couldn't help but notice how the salt and pepper at his temples made him look more distinguished. I liked the laugh lines that appeared on the sides of his mouth. He filled out that suit, looking sexier than any other man in the room.

I swallow and close my eyes.

What the hell am I doing? Scott didn't send me flowers. Tia did. Or my aunt. Or, a flicker of hope, maybe Dad?

Opening my eyes, I pull the little notecard from the envelope and my breathing halts in my chest. The handwriting is neat and tidy, small. Was the guy who delivered the flowers the same who took the message? Or were these flowers purchased in person?

Noelle—

Congratulations on the opening of Primrose Sweets, the Boston edition. It's wonderful to see your signature stamp on the city. I hope to see you soon too. All the best on this exciting new venture.

Scotty

I bite my bottom lip as I reread the words. Why did he send me these gorgeous flowers and sweet note? Because he and my dad are rivals? Because we've always shared a connection, no matter how much time has passed?

Or because he's genuinely happy that I'm here. That I took his advice. And that the last time he saw me, he felt it too. The pull, the chemistry, the desire between us.

I let out a shaky exhale.

Scott Reland belongs to a world I'm trying to distance myself from. First, there's my father. Then, the Sharks franchise. Plus, my ex-boyfriend Chris, now a retired player, who made me realize just how demanding and difficult the life of an NHL wife would be. For years, I've sworn off this type of future. I've committed myself to my studies, to my business.

The last man I should feel a spark for is Scott Reland. Scotty.

But I can't deny that my heart accelerates at the thought.

AFTER I CLOSE for the night, I walk a few streets over to my new apartment. It's a sweet one-bedroom with beat-up wooden floors and exposed brick. The original kind, not the trendy look. I've decorated it simply but it's warm, and as I scrunch my toes into the plush living room carpet, it feels like home.

I pour a glass of wine, kick back on the couch, and prop my feet up on the coffee table. After mindlessly flipping through Netflix recommendations, I work up the nerve to call Scott, wondering if this is still his number since it's been five years since we exchanged contact info.

He answers on the first ring and my heart leaps into my throat. "Welcome to Titletown, Noelle."

I roll my eyes at the term, showcasing Boston's dominance in sports, hockey included. But I'm grinning and my smile comes through in my tone. "Thank you for the warm welcome. The flowers are gorgeous."

"Glad you like them. How are you settling in?"

I look around my apartment. "So far, so good. I'm not far from Faneuil Hall."

"A great part of town. You walk the Freedom Trail yet?"

I chuckle. "Not since I was a kid, but I'm excited to be a tourist while I'm here."

"Good."

I roll my lips together, knowing this is the part of the conversation where I would wrap it up. Except, I don't want to hang up just yet. Not when Scott's voice is the most familiar one I've heard all day.

"Listen," he continues, and I bite my bottom lip, my heart rate increasing, "I'm glad you called. I love that you took my advice and opened up shop here."

I roll my eyes again but I'm fighting back a smile.

"And now that you're here, I'd love to put in an order."

"An order?" I arch an eyebrow.

"Yes, it may be too short notice, but I'm hosting an event at my house this Sunday. It's a baby shower—"

"Baby shower?" I interject. Is Scott having a baby with—who? I haven't heard of him being romantically linked to anyone. My stomach feels unsettled as I consider the thought that he's having a baby with a woman he's not even with. But why should that bother me? Scott is a decade older than me and I'm not even on his radar. And he shouldn't be on mine.

"Yeah, one of the guys on my team, his wife's expecting. We're doing a team thing since our resident party planner, Torsten Hansen, retired," he says the words easily, not like he's putting on airs or tooting his own horn. It strikes me because I don't know if Dad's ever hosted an event that celebrates the team, or one of its members, without their being a media motive behind it. "Noelle?"

I clear my throat. "Yes, sorry. Okay, baby shower cupcakes. Do you know the sex of the baby?"

"A surprise."

"Nice. How many?"

"Three dozen."

"Cool. Any suggestions on design or colors?" I wrack my brain for all the normal questions. I ask them every time I take an order and suddenly, I can't recall the list.

"Whatever you think, Noelle. I trust you."

The words surprise me because even though he's talking about a small matter—cupcakes—he says them with a conviction that speaks to something more.

"Good," I murmur.

"Okay, then. Can I pick them up that morning?"

"Absolutely," I recover. "I'll have them ready for you by 10 a.m."

"I'll see you then. Thanks, Noelle."

"Thank you, Scott. For…everything."

He chuckles and disconnects the call.

I toss my phone down and take another sip of my wine. My head buzzes and an excited nervousness expands in my stomach. My move to Boston was dictated by the timing, the availability of the space, the chance to expand.

But now that I'm here, I'm happy Scott Reland is too.

It's serendipitous.

CHAPTER 2
SCOTT

I t's been one hell of a week, but the Hawks won last night, beating out Chicago, which is always a tough game. Today, I get to kick back with the team, celebrate Yaeger and Vivi, and take it easy. While I offered to host the team baby shower weeks ago, I never anticipated being this excited about it.

But mainly, that's because I get to see Noelle DiSanto.

A few weeks ago, a buddy from New York mentioned that she expanded her bakery to the Boston area and ever since I drove by Primrose Sweets, I haven't been able to get Noelle out of my mind. Ever since our dance over the summer, she'd pop up, unbidden, in random thoughts. And now she's here, in my city, on my turf.

I forced myself to wait a week before sending her flowers. I smile, thinking over our conversation earlier in the week. While I wish she had reached out to me directly about her move, I was still happy she called. Maybe even too happy.

I park my SUV, a Tesla Model X, and stand in front of Primrose Sweets. I gotta hand it to her, it couldn't have been easy getting out from under her father's thumb in New York. But here she is, making her dream come true.

I push into the storefront, a little bell ringing, and admire the beauty behind the counter. Her hair is pulled away from her face, a thick hairband holding it back from her forehead, and still, a few ringlets spring loose.

At the sound of the bell, she glances up. When she sees me, her eyes widen and she backs away from the counter, her fingers fluttering over her unruly curls. I grin.

"Love the space, Noelle." I approach the counter as she walks around it, meeting me in front of the glass display case filled with French pastries and perfectly decorated cupcakes. "You've got quite the selection."

"Thanks, Scotty," she says easily, my old nickname rolling off her tongue like she says it daily and not only when our paths cross at hockey games or fundraising galas. She reaches up on her tippy toes as my palm holds her hip, kissing my cheek in greeting. "And thanks again for the flowers."

"I'm glad you like them."

"I hope you like these." She gestures to the three neatly stacked cupcake boxes on the counter. Carefully, she opens the lid on the top box and a hush falls between us as I scan the cupcakes that are too pretty to eat. Some have details that look like lace, others little white, pink, and blue flowers, and some with bows and bow ties.

"These are magnificent," I tell her truthfully, an echo of awe in my tone.

She blushes and I love that my praise matters to her. But these cupcakes, this bakery, her, they all deserve to be celebrated.

"Thanks, Scott. I know you could have gone anywhere in the city, and it means a lot that you took a chance on me and Primrose."

"Ah, I'd never bet against a DiSanto."

She smirks. "Now I know that's a lie."

I chuckle and tug the boxes toward me. "What do I owe you?"

She shakes her head, wiping her hands on the blue striped apron tied around her waist. "On the house. Just feel free to share Primrose with your friends. I've always found word of mouth to be the best kind of marketing."

I shake my head and pull out my wallet. "If you don't tell me the price, I'll think it's something exorbitant and—"

She places her hand over mine and I stop talking as the heat of her palm, the softness of her skin, seeps into mine.

"Please," I murmur, getting lost in the blue pools of her gaze.

She shakes her head.

I sigh and pluck out a hundred-dollar bill, stuffing it into the tip jar.

"Scotty—" she scolds me, reaching for the jar.

But I grip her hip again and she shifts closer to me, surprised but not pulling away from my touch. I squeeze her hip, knowing I should drop my hold but unable to. Not wanting to. Not now when I know how soft her skin feels.

"Come to the shower."

"What?" A little laugh bursts from her lips. "No, I can't do that."

"Why not?"

She shakes her head but she's fighting a smile. "Well, I'm working."

"You sure that's it?" I ask, wondering if her father gave her some weird rules about not fraternizing with the enemy. I wouldn't put it past him.

"What else would it be?" A challenge flares in her eyes and I back down.

"Well, I'll text you my address. In case you get hungry."

She smirks. "I hope you enjoy the cupcakes."

"Thanks again." I hoist up the boxes.

Noelle follows me to the door and holds it open as I slip outside, a gust of wind whipping past. "Take care, Scott."

"See you around, Noelle," I agree, knowing it will be

much sooner than she thinks. Now that I know she's here, you can bet your ass I'll be a regular at Primrose Sweets.

I pop the trunk of my SUV and place the cupcakes inside. Then, I head back to my house. The decorators and caterers are already present, setting everything up.

When my assistant, Jayde, sees me, she rolls her eyes. "I told you I'd pick up the cupcakes."

"I wanted to get them."

She smacks her lips knowingly but doesn't call me out in front of the crews milling about. Instead, she hands me a stack of papers, a Post-it Note stuck on top with a few numbers I need to call today. "I'm heading out. The bar is going over there." She points to the corner of my den. "The signature drink is a yummy mummy."

I snort. "What the hell is that?"

"I think a cranberry-inspired mimosa."

"Hm."

Jayde takes the cupcake boxes from my hands and sets them down on the table. "The caterer will set these up. A playlist has been curated, flowers will be here shortly. Anything else you need?"

"Nope. You sure you don't want to stick around?"

She wrinkles her nose, her nose ring glinting, as she tries for the blasé, playful demeanor she strives for, but I catch a flash of sadness in her eyes. Jayde isn't talking but I'm pretty sure something went down between my organized, often grumpy assistant and last season's rookie, Reese Keller.

"Nah, I'm good. No plans of baking a bun in the oven anytime soon," she quips, tucking her long, dark hair behind her ears.

"Get out of here then, before I think of something useful for you to do."

"I'm going to dye my hair purple. I'll be unavailable for the rest of the day."

"Yeah? Just don't come back looking like a mermaid; it will mess with this whole goth-emo thing you're trying for."

She flips me her middle finger but then pats my shoulder on the way out of my house.

I turn back to the setting unfolding in my kitchen and living room. I've hired all the necessary components to make today's party a true celebration for Yaeger and Vivi. I know Claire Merrick will be delighted to use my espresso machine. Luca Pandatelli will drink all my good booze. Team captain, Austin Merrick, will try to talk shop and his woman, Chloe, will have to rein him in, reminding him that today is a party.

But I can't help and wonder if they'd all come if I didn't own the Hawks. Will this house ever be filled with people just because? Just for fun?

The thought saddens me because at forty-four, I thought I'd have it together by now. The wife, the kids, the jungle gym in the backyard, and the toys strewn across the floor. Big holiday feasts with too many chairs pulled around the table.

Obviously owning an NHL team is big-time. And I'm not complaining. But it's funny how life works, you know? Because this house has never been filled for a non-team celebration.

Shaking the depressing thoughts away, I refocus my attention to the stack of papers in hand. Then I turn down the hallway, slip behind the desk in my home office, and get to work.

THE TEAM DESCENDS on my house like a bunch of college kids on spring break. Raucous laughter, booming voices, and a shriek of delight over the food spread and beautiful cupcakes, the Hawks and their better halves come bustling through my front door.

"Oh my God! Look at these cupcakes!" Claire shrieks, pulling Vivi over to the dessert display, complete with floral arrangements, tea lights, and rose petals.

"What the fuck is a yummy mummy?" Panda asks his girl, Abbi. She rolls her eyes and leaves him behind as she attaches herself to Chloe's side.

"Scott, this is too much. Thank you. It's, wow, it's incredible." Yaeger appears at my side, pure gratitude shining in his expression.

"Nah, I'm glad I could do it," I tell him truthfully, shaking his outstretched hand and slapping him on the back. "You and Vivi deserve all the happiness." I mean it too. While the start of their marriage was anything but conventional, anyone who looks at them can see the love and devotion they feel for each other. Ever since Vivi ended up in the hospital with a scare regarding the baby during the play-offs last year, I've wanted to do something for the couple that would extend my support to their growing family. The team baby shower seemed like a good idea and the BHH girls, always up for a party, were all over it.

"Thank you, Scott. This is…more than I ever imagined." Vivi smiles softly as she comes to stand beside her husband. She wraps me in a hug, which I return, noting the pride that flares in her man's eyes.

"Can I get you guys a drink?" I offer, suddenly wanting one. There's too much raw emotion in the room. Too many genuine feelings that, not for the first time, I wish I felt for someone. Most of the guys on my team found true partnerships over the last few seasons. Even the guys—ahem, Pandatelli and Easton Scotch—who I never envisioned settling down are now faithfully committed to their women.

Will I ever find that? Will I ever have…this?

"I'm all good. Thanks, though," Yaeger says as Vivi holds up a water with lemon.

"All right. Make sure you try a cupcake. They're from a

new bakery. Primrose Sweets," I shout out Noelle, just the thought of her bringing a smile to my face.

"Ooh, I heard about that place," Claire says. And then, "Hey Scott, can I get a—"

"Help yourself, Claire." I gesture toward the fancy espresso machine I still don't know how to work. Luckily, Claire does.

I grab a beer from the bar and turn to survey the party. The team is in high spirits, still riding the win from last night. Everyone seems settled, secure…happy. I take a swig of my beer, letting the bitter hops wash away the pang of loneliness that flares inside.

I shouldn't feel like this now. Not when I'm surrounded by a group of people in my own home.

Not when I'm fortunate enough to host events like this, with people like these.

But still, the ache persists.

CHAPTER 3
NOELLE

I'm getting ready to close the bakery for the evening, pleased with the nearly empty display case, when the bell chimes.

"Hey there," I call out a greeting over my shoulder. I write down the number of eclairs sold and turn.

A woman in black combat boots with purple streaks running through her black hair holds up a brown paper bag. "I've got something for you."

I bite my lip, frowning. Her words remind me of the flower delivery guy from last week but—"I didn't order takeout."

She rolls her eyes, her winged eyeliner on point. "I know. But Scott figured you'd be hungry." She sets the bag down on the counter. "He can be pushy, but he always means it in the best way possible." She spins to look around the space, her gaze lingering over the café tables, mismatched chairs, and assorted vases and candles on each of the tables. "This place is dope. Good for you, DiSanto. Making your own mark." She turns back toward me.

I sputter out a thank you, trying to place her and if our paths have crossed before. She has a confidence that surprises me because it's so genuine, it's refreshing. This stranger knows exactly who she is and as someone who still struggles to own who I am, it makes me happy to witness. I clear my throat and hold out a hand. "I'm sorry, I don't think we've met."

She grins easily. "Not officially." She shakes my hand. "I'm Jayde, Scott's assistant."

"Oh." I glance at the paper bag, feeling guilty he had her bring food. "You didn't have to bring this."

She waves a hand dismissively. "It's no big deal. I wanted to check out the bakery anyway. I like it."

"Thank you."

She points to the bag. "Scott sent a goat cheese and pine nut kale salad, some mushroom risotto—hope you like mushrooms." She grimaces.

I laugh. "I do."

"Good. And there's some chicken and potatoes."

"Sounds perfect. He didn't have to go through all this trouble. *You* didn't have to go through all this trouble."

She shrugs. "He was worried you'd be hungry, working as much and as late as you must be to get this up and running."

"That was very thoughtful of him," I murmur.

"He's a thoughtful guy," she says it as a reflex, but I hear the truth underlining her words. It seems like she genuinely likes working for Scott, doing all the last-minute things he must toss her way. My father has had four assistants in the past eight years, with most of them putting in their notice at the two-year mark, too fed up and overwhelmed to continue with his demanding asks and shifting moods. Only my mom could manage them, although they grew exponentially worse after she passed.

"Here." I place some cupcakes in a box. "Take these home with you."

She smiles and it's bright. "Thanks, Noelle. I'll see ya around."

"Uh, sure," I say quickly, hoping she tells her friends about Primrose.

I watch Jayde leave the shop. Once the door closes, I flip the sign to closed. My stomach rumbles and I laugh to myself. I guess Scott was right; I am hungry. I take the bag to one of the café tables, with an oblong vase and a single white flower, and open my dinner.

Acoustic music plays in the background as I eat by myself, wondering what it would be like to share this meal with someone else. With a partner. For a flicker, Scott pops into my mind but I push the image away.

I know what a life in the NHL world entails and after living it for my entire life as my father's daughter, and then briefly as Chris's girlfriend, it's not a life I want. I want…this.

The peaceful quiet of my bakery after a long day's work. The simplicity of knowing that when I go home tonight, there's nothing demanding I must take care of. The certainty that tomorrow, I get to bake sweet treats for others to enjoy with their loved ones.

I like my routine and rituals. I like simplicity and authenticity. Since moving to Boston, I've missed New York and my bakery, but not the demands that come with being my father's daughter.

Here, I'm just a bakery owner, hustling to get my business off the ground. I bite into the mushroom risotto and moan. I like my new identity more than I thought possible. I like my new world too, even if Scott's presence keeps me tied to hockey in Boston.

When I finish my dinner, I shoot him a text.

NOELLE

You didn't have to send your assistant.

SCOTT

I would have come myself, but the party was
going strong. Worried you were hungry.

NOELLE

Dinner was delicious. Thank you.

SCOTT

Glad you ate.

NOELLE

You're spoiling me. I'm not used to this kind
of treatment.

SCOTT

You should be.

A shiver rolls down my spine. Is there a promise behind his words? Do I want there to be?

SCOTT

You home yet?

I look around the empty bakery and out the window, to the night sky and quiet street.

NOELLE

Not yet. Leaving soon.

A few minutes tick by and then—

SCOTT

Will you let me know when you're home? I'll
worry otherwise.

I bite my lip. He'll worry because…he's a good guy who would worry about any woman he knows leaving a bakery late at night in Boston? Probably. Still, my heart flutters at the thought that he worries about *me*.

I groan. What is wrong with me? Scott Reland is Daddy's biggest rival. He's also a decade older than me and has known me for years. He probably views me as a kid he needs to keep an eye on, as someone having their first experience away from their safe haven, in this case, New York.

I get a grip on my wayward thoughts and message back an appropriate response.

NOELLE

Sure.

SCOTT

I'm serious, Noelle. Please let me know when you're home or if you need a ride.

And I soften again.

NOELLE

I will.

I finish my closing tasks and step out into the cold winter night. I look up and book it to my car, blasting the heat and holding my fingers next to the vents. Then, I drive home, change into pajamas, slide on my slippers, and pour a glass of red wine.

I sit on the couch, blow out a deep breath, and text Scott.

NOELLE

I'm home.

A second later, my phone rings and I try to quell the bubble of excitement that expands in my stomach when I read his name on the screen.

"Hello?" I answer.

"Noelle." His voice is rich and warm. Soothing. "How was your day?"

I chuckle. "Sold more pastries than I was expecting so it was pretty great. How was the shower?"

"It was...good. Better than I anticipated."

I take a sip of my wine, surprised by his honesty. "You didn't think it'd be a success?"

He chortles. "No, I mean, I knew the party would be fine. It was more...the environment. I never know at these things if the guys are here because I'm the owner and invited them or because they really want to be here. Not out of obligation."

I tip my head back and think that over. "I don't think my father's ever considered that."

"I doubt it," he agrees, and there's no malice in his tone. "Your dad's from a different generation. One who focuses on—"

"Respect."

"Exactly."

"Don't you want to be respected?" I wonder.

"Of course. But more for the kind of person I am than the type of job I have." Scott says it simply, like it's obvious. And once I think over the words, it is the obvious choice. I doubt many people realize that.

"I like that. The fact that you're thinking this much about it, I'm sure your team was there because they wanted to be."

"It felt that way today," he admits, stifling a yawn.

"Tired? Too much fun at a baby shower?"

"Sugar crash. The cupcakes were a hit."

I smile, pleased that he enjoyed them. "I'm glad. I was nervous about expanding to another city but so far, Boston's been good to me."

"How've you been generating business?" His tone changes, focused on business now.

It's so much like Dad, I smile.

"Mostly word of mouth. I've tossed some money at Instagram to attract a younger crowd. Hit up the college campuses too."

"That was smart. College kids love a coffee shop, bakery. But you don't want them taking up your tables all day, studying, for a latte."

I snort. "True. But right now, I don't mind."

"Are you set up to produce more cupcakes? On a larger scale?"

Where is he going with this? "Yes, the kitchen is fully

operational and equipped at an industrial level. Right now, it's just me, but in a city like Boston, I'm sure I can find qualified support. I'm beginning interviews next week."

"Good," he responds. Then, he's quiet, and it's as if I can hear his mind turning over ideas. "What about a pop-up shop?"

"A pop up—"

"At The Meadows."

My heart thunks and I place down my wine glass. Is he saying what I think he's saying? No way. "Are you asking if I want to have a pop-up stand at the arena? During hockey games?" I ask slowly, needing full confirmation before I believe him.

"Exactly."

What? I shift forward, perched on the edge of the couch. That would make my business boom, and he knows it. Excitement whirls around me as I process this opportunity. Followed quickly by a pang that Dad never offered me a chance like this in New York.

I chase that feeling away by focusing on this conversation, Boston, Scott.

"Wow! You're serious?" I repeat.

He chuckles. "Yes. There's only one caveat."

Some of my excitement simmers. "What?"

"You've gotta do them in Hawks colors. Blue and white."

I groan. Dad is going to lose his mind if he learns that I'm selling Hawks cupcakes at The Meadows. He'll see it as a sign of…disrespect.

"It's a great opportunity, Noelle."

"I know. It's just…"

"Your father?" he correctly guesses.

"He won't understand it."

"This isn't personal, it's business. Yours. And mine. People come to The Meadows, they come for the Hawks."

Of course, he's right. And this is an incredible opportunity for me, one to solidify my bakery in Boston. I'd be a fool to turn it down, and still, I waver.

Is he offering me this chance to get back at Dad for something? To use my budding friendship with him as ammunition against my father?

"Think it over," he says slowly, his tone neutral. "In fact, why don't you come to The Meadows this week? I'll show you around, we can talk things over, and you can see if it's something you might be interested in."

At the lack of judgment in his tone, I feel even worse. The man's offering me a huge opportunity to introduce my product to a new market and I'm waffling.

I clear my throat. "Okay. Sure, that sounds good."

"Good. How's Tuesday?"

I wrack my brain to make sure I can dip out of the bakery early on Tuesday. "I can close early. Is 4 p.m. okay?"

"I'll see you then," he agrees.

"Thank you, Scott."

"Have a good night, Noelle."

I hang up the phone and swipe up my wine glass. I sip it slowly, mentally replaying my conversation with Scott. Since I've arrived in Boston, he's been nothing but kind, considerate, and thoughtful.

Still, I know Daddy will dislike my spending time with him. But if I'm trying to build my brand and grow my business, don't I need to make smart decisions?

If I'm serious about not running the Sharks empire, don't I need to ensure the success of Primrose Sweets?

CHAPTER 4
SCOTT

"I'm hanging up my skates," Noah Scotch, a player I've watched grow up, grow into a man while playing for the Hawks, announces.

I look up from my laptop, beckoning him to come farther into my office. I stand to shake his hand. "What's going on?"

He heaves out an exhale and slumps into the chair across from my desk. "I'm done, Scott. Doc doesn't think my knee is going to heal a hundred percent and honestly, I'm not interested in shredding up my body for a few more years. I'm getting older—"

"You're thirty-five," I remind him.

He smirks. "I had a great career."

"You did," I agree, waiting for him to clue me in on why he's taking this news as well as he is.

"I have an even better family. Indy's pregnant."

"What?" Surprise, closely followed by genuine happiness for my player, my friend, rolls through me. "Congratulations, Scotch!" I walk to the bar in the corner and pour us two glasses of scotch. I pass one to him and we clink glasses. Taking a sip, I savor the smooth, bold flavor as it warms me from the inside out. "You and Indy aren't wasting any time. Jesus, how old is Emmaline?"

"Almost eighteen months," he chuckles. "It was a surprise. But the best kind. We've decided to hold off on a big wedding. We're just going to do something small—city hall and dinner. And then, when Indy isn't puking her guts up, we'll do a big party sometime next year."

I nod, sipping my scotch. "You've got it all planned out."

"Hardly," he scoffs. "All I know is, my knee is shot. I don't have the same speed, the agility, or the confidence when I get out on the ice. And if I don't have that, I'm more prone to—"

"Injury."

"Can't risk it, Scott. Not when my girls rely on me," he answers easily, at peace with his decision.

"Wow, I'm, well… I wasn't sure how your recovery would be. I'm more surprised by your acceptance of things than I am by your decision. But I'm glad to see you're okay with this. Really. Of course, you'll be missed."

He smiles. "My contract was ending this year anyway. I'll see out the season."

"And then?"

He bites the corner of his mouth and I lift my eyebrows.

"Listen, we've always been tighter than just owner-player," he says.

The words ease some of the tension I carry between my shoulder blades. All these years, and I still don't have the tight circle of trust, of friends, that I see others, even my players, have formed. Hearing Scotch admit that our relationship is deeper than our professions is a relief. I nod, waving for him to continue.

"The Tennessee Thunderbolts are crumbling."

"The Tennessee Thunderbolts are for sale."

His expression clears and he nods, taking a swig of his scotch.

I arch an eyebrow, reading between the lines as the pieces click together. "You thinking of buying the team?"

He snorts. "You don't pay me that well, Scott."

I grin. "But—?"

"Torsten and Rielle, Torsten's family, are in negotiations to buy the team outright."

I whistle but inside, I'm happy for my former defenseman. "He's got a keen eye for good bets," I murmur, recalling when he married Rielle.

"Jeremiah and I are going to be small, very small, shareholders and head up the coaching," Scotch continues, surprising me again.

"You're gonna work, *coach*, with your father-in-law?" For an instant, DiSanto pops into my mind, but I shake the thought away. Guy's never going to be part of my family and if he was, he'd probably try to poison me first.

"You know Jem. I lucked out in the in-law department."

"You sure as hell did. And Jeremiah's career, being in the Hall of Fame, will lend some credibility to your management."

"Exactly," Noah agrees. "We got the old blood and the young blood."

I chuckle. "Don't let him hear you say that." I finish my drink and clunk the glass down on my desk. The sound somehow rings with a finality I wasn't expecting. Suddenly, I feel strangely emotional at the thought of Scotch leaving, of starting the next chapter of his life, his career, in Tennessee and not Boston. "You're going to make one hell of a coach."

His brown eyes are warm, brimming with a gratitude I feel bone-deep when he looks straight at me. "I'd never have made it this far without you, Scott. The Hawks, the culture here, you built a family. One I've always been grateful, honored, to be a part of." He stands and holds out his hand.

I round my desk and shake his hand, pulling him into a hug. "Proud of you, Noah."

"Thank you. But go easy on us on the ice, yeah?"

I snort, slapping his shoulder. "I'm glad you came to talk to me about this."

"You're the only person, outside of the people involved, who know anything."

"I won't say a word."

"I know. I just…wanted to make sure you're okay with it. Don't feel blindsided."

His thoughtfulness is touching. "You have my blessing."

Scotch laughs. "Good. And Indy and I haven't shared about the baby yet either. It's…early days."

"I understand. I'm happy for you, man. You're building a beautiful life."

"Thanks, Scott. You, uh, you seeing anyone?" he asks the question more curiously than anything else.

"Nothing serious," I play it off, the way I always do. There hasn't been a serious woman in my life in years. Most of them see dollar signs or status when they look at me and that gets old real fast. Like Noelle and I spoke about, I want to be recognized, appreciated, for the person I am more than anything else. I guess that extends to all aspects of my life.

"One day the right one will come along." He places his glass on my desk.

"We'll see." I shrug, walking him toward the office door. "If you need any help as you navigate this deal, reach out. Buck," I reference the current Bolts owner, "and I go way back."

"Really?"

"Yep. He was tight with my old man. I've known him since I was a kid."

"Thank you. I appreciate that." He shakes my hand. When he opens the door, Jayde is walking by. She shoots us a curious look, a smirk glancing off her mouth as her gaze zeros in on the empty tumblers. Mentally, I groan, knowing she's going to ask me a million questions later.

"Stick with the PT," I remind him.

He grins. "Sure thing, Scott. I'll see you at the game."

I nod and stand in the doorframe, watching as Noah Scotch walks down the hallway for one of the last times as a Hawk. He stops to chat with random office staff. He's been a part of this franchise for so long that almost everyone knows, and adores, him.

It will be tough to lose him, but I also feel a swell of pride for the player, the man, he's become. The Thunderbolts will be lucky to have him, just like I was.

I POLISH off my post-workout smoothie and sit back at my desk, ready to dive into the list of calls and urgent emails Jayde flagged for me. My office phone rings and I answer.

"Yeah?"

"Rick DiSanto is on line two."

Rick? "What's he want?"

Jayde scoffs. "How would I know?"

If she wasn't so damn good at her job, I'd fire her for the grief she gives me. I swear, she's worse than a teenage daughter. "Patch him through."

"Maybe drink another scotch to fortify yourself for the call."

Fine, I keep her around for her humor. She's one of the only people in my life who mouths off to me and I think it's mainly because she can't help herself, not because she knows I secretly get a kick out of it. "I'm ready for him, Rocky." I toss out her nickname since she's a bit of a brawler, more into Muay Thai than hockey.

I hear the beep, followed by a gruff voice. "Scott."

"Hi, Rick, how are you?" I lean back in my chair.

"What's this nonsense of you sending Noelle flowers?"

Oh, brother. How the hell did he find out? Did Noelle tell him? "Just welcoming her to Boston."

"She's too smart to fall for your bullshit," he advises, a thread of anger in his tone.

"No bullshit, Rick. Just reaching out, in case she needs anything. Thought you'd be glad."

"Nah, you knew I wouldn't like it. Noelle belongs in New York. She's a Shark. One day, not too far in the future, all of this, everything I've built, will be hers. I don't need her getting silly ideas and thinking about putting down roots in Boston."

"Silly ideas?" I question. Does he mean about the pop-up shop? Or has he caught onto my attraction to Noelle? Because there's no hiding that one. Not when just seeing her spikes my blood pressure.

"Owning a bakery," he heaves out, as if I'm dense for not following along.

I frown, sitting up straight in my chair. "From what I hear, her location in New York is doing pretty well. And Boston is off to a solid start."

"Yeah? And how do you think she got the money to start up this little hobby?"

I bristle at his insinuation. At both of them. "I'm guessing all the work she's done for the Sharks, probably without ever receiving fair pay, helped as an initial investment. And I don't think this is a hobby. She seems to be thriving in her business. Running it as a business."

He swears. This time, when he speaks, his tone is less gruff. It's firm and clear and glacial. "So now you know more about my daughter than me, Reland? What the hell are you playing at?"

I close my eyes, knowing I shouldn't take the bait. But— "Maybe you don't know Noelle as well you think you do."

He swears at me. "Leave my daughter out of whatever

shit you're stirring. She's too smart to fall for it and I won't stand for it."

Then, he hangs up the phone and I'm left listening to the dial tone.

Shit. He's serious. He thinks I'm trying to…manipulate Noelle? The thought angers me because I'd never do something stupid and shady like that. The fact that Rick jumped to that conclusion gives me pause that maybe he would, or has, done something similar. Bitterness explodes on my tongue, my conversation with him leaving behind a bad taste.

Poor Noelle, having to put up with his shit for so long. No wonder she's in Boston, trying to carve out a niche for herself. Even though I already offered to help, I'm now more committed to convincing her that the pop-up shop is in her best interest. Frankly, it is. And I don't give a shit what Rick thinks about that.

A knock on my office door has me looking up. "Yeah?"

Jayde pops her head in.

"You look like an angry Madam Mim," I tell her, noting the purple hair.

Her eyebrows pull together as she plops down across from my desk. "Who?" She places a Starbucks in front of me, tipping a second cup to her mouth.

"Madam Mim," I repeat. "From *The Sword in the Stone*."

She looks at me like I've grown a third eyeball.

"Disney," I say, hoping to jog her memory.

She places down her mocha and holds up a finger. Pulling out her phone, she taps on the screen. Then, she bursts into laughter. "Oh my God," she wheezes, showing me the screen with an image of Madam Mim. "This movie is from the sixties! How the hell old are you, Scott?"

I give her a look. She knows damn well that I'm forty-four.

"You're dating yourself. Big time," she continues.

"I hate you," I mumble, taking a sip of my cappuccino.

She grins. "You'd die without me."

"The size of your ego, given these surroundings"—I gesture to the arena at large—"always manages to impress me."

She stacks her feet off the corner of my desk. "I'm good at what I do. Now, let's talk about the big block of time on your calendar starting tomorrow. Four p.m.?"

"You can take off early tomorrow."

"Because…?"

"I don't need you."

Slowly, Jayde smiles. I like to pretend it's grotesque but really, when Jayde smiles, it's breathtaking. Her golden-brown eyes shimmer, and she looks a hell of a lot more innocent than she is. "You've got a date."

"I don't."

"With Noelle DiSanto!" She points at me, accusingly.

"It's work-related."

She chuckles with glee. "Oh my God! This is the best!" She removes her ankles from my desk and sits straight. "You like her!"

"I've always liked her," I reply, my face devoid of emotion.

"Nope." The little ball buster shakes her head. "You *really* like her."

"I want her to open a pop-up cupcake shop here, at the arena."

Jayde chews her bottom lip, thinking that over. "That's a great idea. It will provide another option for fans and help get the word out about her bakery."

"Exactly."

"When is she starting?"

"She's needing some…convincing," I say delicately.

Jayde's eyebrows fly off her face, disappearing into the curtain of bangs that always fall into her eyes. "She's not sure if she's going to do it?" Before I can answer, she continues. "Of course, it's her dad, isn't it?"

I groan. "I'm going to fire you one of these days."

"For being smart?"

"For being nosy."

She shrugs. "You wouldn't last a week."

I don't say anything because…she's probably right. Jayde's been with me since reluctantly doing an internship her aunt, one of the office staff, begged me to give her three years ago. As soon as I realized her bad attitude was mostly related to her lack of a challenge, I started tossing things her way. The more I gave her, the better she delivered. She's been my assistant ever since, part-time until she finished college last year, and now, full-time.

"For what it's worth," Jayde says, standing, "I hope she says yes. And I'm booking a nail appointment for tomorrow if you're sure you don't need me."

I wave a hand at her and wait until she leaves the office.

Then I release a shaky breath, my stomach swirling with anticipation and a sliver of hope for tomorrow.

I hope she says yes too.

CHAPTER 5
NOELLE

"It's an opportunity," I remind Dad as I park in the lot of The Meadows.

"An opportunity to use my own daughter against me," Dad grumbles.

Clearly, telling him about the pop-up shop Scott offered was a huge mistake. I knew it before I opened my mouth and still, the small part of me that craves his approval, made the words tumble out. *Obey your father, Noelle.* Why is that the only thing I can hear clearly in Mom's voice? Why do I still need Dad's blessing for things that have nothing to do with him? And why does his reaction, fully expected, still hurt? I wish he could be happy for *me* instead of viewing everything through a lens that circles back to the Sharks.

"I think it will be good for Primrose, which is good for *me*," I remind him, pointing out that important detail.

"But the Sharks are—"

"Dad, how many times have we gone through this? I don't want to manage the Sharks."

"You could still be involved," he snaps back. "Take your rightful position—"

"There's nothing right about nepotism," I remind him.

He swears and I can picture him pinching the bridge of his nose, his eyes darting around the room in search of where he left his jacket and the cigar tucked into the inside pocket. "Noelle, you're smart, you're a go-getter, you can manage the team."

I close my eyes and sigh. "Thanks, Daddy. But I don't want to. I want to give *this* a shot. I love baking," I say it softly, hoping my lack of attitude will demonstrate the truth of my words. "And my bakery honors Mom. Running Primrose makes me feel close to her."

Dad sighs, the sound resigned. "All right, we'll see. I'll talk to you later. Love you, Noelle."

"Love you too," I back down immediately. How can I not? The giant, the legend, of New York City is my dad. And sure, he's rough around the edges, but he's been present every day of my life, ensuring that I have everything I need. When Mom passed, he stepped up big time, learning to braid my hair and pack my lunchboxes. He's by no means warm and cuddly, but he's been my protector since day one. "'Bye, Daddy." I hang up the phone and toss it into my purse.

I shake off my nerves, climb out of my car, and square my shoulders. Then, I stride toward the entrance of The Meadows, viewing it the same way I've viewed hockey arenas my entire life: with a little bit of awe, a dash of skepticism, and the nostalgic feeling of childhood.

Entering the space, the warmth of the culture immediately wraps around me. As someone who has spent my growing years in arenas across the country, I can feel the energy immediately. The culture is formed by the owner, by the people he or she hires as management. My first impression is that Scott chose smartly because the two janitors I pass in the hallways as well as the receptionist when I enter the office space all wish me a good afternoon with genuine smiles.

"How can I help you?" the receptionist asks.

"Hi. I'm here to see Scott. My name is Noelle—"

"DiSanto," she finishes for me, standing from her seat. She extends her hand which I shake. "I haven't seen you in years. Do you remember me? Peggy." When she smiles, the corners of her eyes crinkle and an old memory floats through my mind.

"From the St. Louis game," I murmur, trying to catch the memory.

Peggy laughs. "I thought your father was going to blow a gasket when he realized just how many sweets you had that game."

I grin, recalling the cotton candy and entire box of mini-donuts I inhaled. "I had a horrible stomachache all night," I laugh.

"How's your dad doing?"

"Pretty good. Things in New York are intense at the moment," I admit.

Peggy nods sympathetically. "Trading Devon Hardt must have been tough."

"It was," I say quietly. Devon had been one of Dad's star players for a decade. Unfortunately, an injury, an end of contract, and a new direction for the team meant that Devon was traded, gutting him almost as much as Dad.

"Scott's waiting for you," Peggy offers. "I can walk you to his office," she says just as her phone rings.

"It's no worries. Which door?"

She points down the hallway. "Fourth on the right." She picks up the phone. "Good afternoon—"

I wave in farewell and enter the hallway. The design is contemporary, completely different than the offices I'm used to in New York. While Dad's style is more traditional—think rich mahogany and plush carpets—Scott's offices are contemporary with trendy embellishments that offer a refreshing, energetic vibe. Abstract artwork hangs on the walls with bright pops of color. The wide-planked hardwood floor is fashioned in a herringbone pattern that is eye-catching without being overkill. This is a space where creativity is encouraged, where new ideas are discussed, where passion not just for the business, but for the entire institution, burns.

I lift my hand and knock on his door.

"Come in," he calls out and I push inside, the floor-to-ceiling windows behind his desk giving me the most beautiful view of downtown Boston.

Scott looks up from his computer and a wide smile crosses his face, his green eyes blazing. Dressed in a white V-neck, his tanned skin from his recent trip to the Caribbean—I fully admit to stalking his social media—glows. A blazer rests on the back of his chair, a colorful pocket square peeking out of the pocket.

He stands and comes to greet me.

"Noelle, glad you could make it." He embraces me, kissing my cheek. The tip of his nose glides along my skin, making me shiver as I breathe in his scent, a clean, fresh cologne, like pine trees in winter and snow-filled mountain caps.

"Hi, Scotty," I quip, trying to find my equilibrium as his office, his presence, affects me. What is it about Scott Reland that makes me feel young yet seen? Innocent yet appreciated.

His gaze doesn't waver as he steps back. His hand rests lightly against my back, his palm splayed wide, as he guides me to a chair.

I sink into the leather cushion, placing my purse on the floor beside me. While I wait for him to round his desk, he surprises me by sitting in the chair next to mine. He leans back and casually crosses his legs, one ankle resting over his other knee, like we're old friends about to settle in for a catch-up session instead of a business meeting.

But was this only ever about business?

I flush at the thought and Scott takes note, the corners of his mouth curling.

"How's the bakery?" Before I can answer, he leans

forward, his eyes narrowing. "Would you like a coffee? Water?"

I shake my head. "I'm fine, thanks. And Primrose is great. Our opening month exceeded my expectations and I've hired two people this week, one to work in the kitchen with me, early mornings, and the other to manage the register. I'm hoping he'll be able to do more of the afternoon and evening shifts." I'm pleased with how Bostonians have welcomed Primrose, in fact, I'm pleased with my move to Boston, however temporary it may be.

But I've been hesitant to bask in that happy glow. Mainly because it's still early days and I don't want to get ahead of myself. But also because Dad's been adamant about needing my help, needing me to take on a leadership role, in New York. My stomach tightens, uncomfortable at the thought, and I focus back on Scott and the flicker of pride in his green eyes.

"Good for you, Noelle. I'm happy to hear it. So, you're up for expanding operations?"

"Definitely," I say. "It's just the Hawks colors that are throwing me for a loop."

He smirks. "Because of the optics?"

"There's that," I say, knowing he knows exactly what the issue is. My dad. If I'm seen, publicly, supporting the Hawks, even in a business capacity, over the Sharks, Dad will never hear the end of it. I'm sure he'll question my loyalty, my commitment to the Sharks and the future role he's concocting for me in the organization. If there's one thing that truly bothers me, it's the question of loyalty. Mom had it in spades and as her daughter, I would never want to disappoint her memory by having Dad think I'm disloyal to our family. "Everyone assumes I'm going to take over for Dad one day."

"True," Scott says simply, his expression neutral.

"Can you imagine how it will look? Selling cupcakes, fashioning treats, for the Hawks, for The Meadows?"

Scott shrugs. "So, do it for the Sharks instead? I'm sure your father would love to have you back in the city."

I dip my head at the nonchalance in his tone. Dad's never offered me the opportunity to expand my operations within the arena.

"Noelle," Scott's voice is low. He's closer now, his hand covering mine, the weight of it curling my palm over my knee.

I glance up, noting the tightness in his jaw, the seriousness of his gaze. A moment ago, they were light and playful. Now, they're dark, forest green, and intense.

"I want this to be an opportunity for you. If you want to make a serious go of this, of the bakeries, of opening more locations and expanding your business, then you should throw all your weight behind it. Go all in so you're never left wondering what could have been. I know what your dad intends for you. But is that what you want for yourself?"

I blink, feeling my cheeks turn rosy again.

"Don't answer that," Scott murmurs, one side of his mouth tugging up. "Unless you want to."

I smile and flip my hand over, pressing our palms together. Scott draws in a breath, his eyes narrowing as he studies me.

"I want to say yes," I murmur. The air around us has shifted, a tension that wasn't previously present making itself known. My stomach coils and my heart rate spikes. Each inhale contains traces of Scott's cologne and his exhales feather over my collarbone. We're so close that we've crossed the line of a business meeting and are beginning to veer past flirty friendship as well.

"Then say yes." His tone is low, so deep it tugs in my lower abdomen. "But because you want to. Only because you want it."

His eyes are trained on mine, brimming with too many contradictions to sort through. His jawline is severe, his nostrils flaring slightly. It feels like we're not talking about cupcakes at all anymore.

My mouth grows dry, and I wet my lips, Scott's eyes darting to take in the movement, his fingers curling over mine.

"What do you want, Noelle?"

"Yes," I murmur. "I'd like to try a pop-up shop."

He holds my hand tightly for a beat, not blinking, and then he exhales, long and ragged. Scott nods once and backs away, as if coming to some type of conclusion, as if my decision marked the end of the moment.

The loss of his touch is replaced by a chill and my head spins, confused. Did I read into that? Was he only being so, what's the right word?—*confounding*—because he wanted me to say yes?

Is all of this only about cupcakes? Or was he asking for something more?

"Yes," he says, and for a second, I think he's answered my silent thought. "I'm glad you're going to give it a shot. I'd love to have you here." The "l" word in his voice does strange things to my insides, and I drop my head to release a shuddering breath.

What the hell is happening? Why am I reacting this way?

To Scott! A man so firmly entrenched in the hockey world, in the industry, that his entire future is mapped out with more of my past.

Flustered, I bend to retrieve my purse. I need to go. I have to think all of this over from the safety of my bakery, or my couch. With wine. Red wine.

"I made reservations for an early dinner," his voice cuts through my thoughts, smooth and unhurried. "Don't rush off."

I look up to find him leaning against his desk. His ankles are crossed, his arms folded across his chest. While I expect to see amusement in his eyes, they're shadowed with earnestness.

"Please," he adds, confusing me further. "Let me take you to eat. I think you'll enjoy it."

Inwardly, I groan. Because I'm already enjoying this, whatever the hell *this* is, more than I should. More than I want to. But denying it, lying to myself, doesn't make it any less true. I want to spend time with Scott. I like getting to see this side of him, the man outside of the hockey arena.

So, for the second time in a handful of minutes, I compose myself. I tilt my head as I study him. Nothing about his demeanor implies that this is some ridiculous ruse to piss off my father. Instead, his eyes hold mine with a hunger that I know well. I feel it expanding in my stomach, unraveling down my limbs like spools of ribbon. Desire.

"Yes," I say clearly.

Scott smiles and moves to pull on his blazer.

I stand, clutching my purse.

"I'll drive," he says.

I suck in a breath. We've now crossed flirty friendship as well. I think Scott Reland and I are firmly moving into date territory.

I'm not sure what to make of that because…it's all wrong.

I don't date men in my father's world. Not anymore.

I don't allow myself to tangle up with men I have a business arrangement with. And as of ten minutes ago, I have one with Scott.

I don't blur lines. I keep things simple, straightforward, orderly.

Scott's hand shadows my back again and my stomach plummets.

There is nothing simple or orderly about my feelings for Scott.

Still, I let him guide me through the door, past a surprised Peggy, and into a private portion of a parking garage to his new Tesla. I slip into the passenger seat, breathe in the scent of Scott beside me, and don't look back.

Because Scott was right. I need to say yes for me, for what I want.

And right now, I want to explore whatever the hell this is between us.

CHAPTER 6
SCOTT

She's quiet on the drive to the restaurant. Lost in her thoughts. Her head is tipped pensively, eyes trained out the window.

I want to reach over, reach for her hand, physically connect with her to let her know, I get it. I know what it's like wanting the approval of a parent, of a loved one, of desperately seeking the knowledge that they're on your side no matter what. It's even worse for only children, which Noelle and I both are.

But I don't know Noelle that well. Sure, we've been in the same circles for years but not counting two real conversations, our interactions have always been easy and casual. The things I want to discuss with her, hell the things I want to *do* with her, are new territory for us. The desire I feel for her, its intensity, its constant presence since she moved to Boston, is new territory for *me*.

"Hope you like Italian," I quip, cutting the silence.

She turns toward me, a sheepish grin on her face. "I'm an Italian-American from New York, Scott. I hope your Italian can measure up."

"I'm taking you to the North End, Noelle. You haven't tried Italian-American until you've been here."

She smirks, her eyes lighting. "You're pretty sure of yourself."

I snicker. "I learned early on, the more you say something with confidence, the more others tend to believe it."

"So, you shoot off the hip?" An arched eyebrow.

"Never. Educated guesses and then"—I flash her a grin—"fake it 'til you make it, right?"

"Right." She shakes her head. "I forgot how easy it is to talk to you. How…"

When she trails off, I turn to look at her. "Fun?"

Her mouth curves into a smile as I focus back on the road, slowing down as we hit some run-of-the-mill traffic. The Big Dig construction project that ran through the city for over fifteen years flickers through my mind and I stifle a laugh, hoping she's not going to say *old*. Because that traffic, the bane of my existence, was before she had a driver's license.

"Fun," she agrees and I laugh.

"Did you think I'd be a stuffy, old guy now?"

"You're not *that* old."

"Thanks."

She giggles and shakes her head, her ringlets bouncing around her face. Damn, she's angelic. "I guess I thought you'd be more…serious, intense."

I lift a wry eyebrow.

"About work," she clarifies. "Dad is busy, locked into the team, one-hundred percent of the time. It's part of the reason why Mom and I were so close; it was usually just the two of us. And here you are, taking me to dinner just because…"

"I don't remember your mom. I never met her," I say quietly. Mrs. DiSanto passed before I started with the Hawks. "But I heard she was always laughing."

Noelle smiles. "Yeah, I miss her. Dad's great but Mom was just more…balanced. She was the one who kept everything going, who kept Dad grounded. She truly enjoyed her life. I wish I was more like that, but Dad rubbed off on me. I'm too focused, driven. I like the fast pace of city life and new challenges. Sometimes, I don't even know how to relax."

I tip my chin sympathetically. "I'm with you there. It's easier for me now, but when I first bought the Hawks, it was hard for me to take a day off, never mind something radical, like going on vacation. Like your dad, mine groomed me for this role."

"Your dad owned the Hawks?" Surprise laces her tone and I spare her a glance.

"You don't know this story?"

She shakes her head, her gaze curious.

I laugh lightly and slide my hand over the top of the steering wheel. "My dad was a baseball guy. Always has been. My childhood was spent in Pee Wee ball, pitching camps, clinics and conditioning. I breathed baseball. But my heart wasn't in it. It was his dream, not mine. When I was in high school, our ice hockey team needed an extra player to qualify for some tournament. Some of my friends were on the team and asked me if I'd join, so I did. And that was it."

"That was it?"

"I never looked back. Went all in on hockey."

"And your dad?"

"I think he was disappointed, but not angry or anything. That came later." I give her a soft smile. "When he passed his ownership of the Boston Eagles baseball team to me."

She sucks in a sharp exhale, and I know she's anticipating what comes next. It was a dark time in my family's history, and while it wasn't my best decision in many ways, in others, it's the greatest choice I've ever made.

"The Hawks franchise was still small then. They weren't a powerhouse, still getting off the ground. My ownership in the Eagles was small, about ten percent. Around that time, leadership was changing, doping was more prevalent, the politics of it all, the behind-the-scenes was messy as hell. It's one of the reasons Dad called me up early. He had some health concerns and the stress of it was getting to him." I pause, recalling my dad's strong jawline, his broad shoulders, how it once felt to sit atop of them, like I was on top of the world. "My heart wasn't in it, not from the start. I tried, really tried, but my vision wasn't in line with the rest. I wanted to build a solid team, even if that meant taking losses."

"And everyone else was worried about winning."

"Exactly. One night, having a few more drinks than I should have, I sat down at a poker game."

Noelle groans and I shake my head.

"Stakes were my ten percent in the Eagles for fifty-one percent of the Hawks. The other guy was being coached by his uncle. At the time, it was a no-brainer, the Eagles were worth a hell of a lot more money, no one had ever heard of the Hawks. Back then, hockey in Boston meant the New England Bears. The Hawks were a relatively new team, unknown talent, and on the surface, it didn't seem like much."

"But you knew."

I nod. "And I wanted it. That game was the best and worst decision I ever made. I threw it on purpose, let my opponent think he got one over on me. Went home, slept off my hangover, broke my father's heart."

Noelle sighs, her expression sympathetic. She reaches over and takes my hand, her touch gentle, sweet. "I'm sorry, Scott."

"Don't be," I assure her, turning my palm upward to press against hers. "That Monday, I got to work. And I never looked back." I shoot her a smirk and tighten my hold on her fingers. "That's a bit of advice I always pass along. Once you take a decision, go all in. Don't second-guess yourself, don't waver. Make a complete go of it. Never wonder what could have been because that only leads to regrets."

Noelle chews her bottom lip, slowly nodding. When she meets my gaze, her eyes are shaded with concern. "And your dad?"

"Forgave me. Eventually," I tack on. "I'm not going to lie and say our relationship wasn't strained. For years, it was. Probably more so because I felt guilty. And I'll never get those years back with him, which is something I have to live with. But a few months before he passed, I went to visit him. The Hawks had all but eaten up the Eagles by then. We were dominating in the sports world, all over the media, a household name."

Noelle smiles, her expression a mix of awe and pride that my ego likes.

"And he told me I made the right decision, for my life. That he couldn't see it at the time because it felt like a betrayal, it felt like a reckless, stupid thing his kid did drunk. But now, he was proud of the team I built, of the vision I was creating. He came to all our games that season. When he passed in the summer, we were on good terms, and I know he didn't hold my decision against me."

"Good. I'm glad you got that closure." She squeezes my fingers once before letting go of my hand. "I don't know if my dad would ever feel that way."

"Gotta give him a chance," I advise.

She wrinkles her nose, skeptical.

"I know it doesn't feel that way now. You're in the midst of it and it's a lot of pressure, a lot of expectations. All I'm saying is, whatever you decide to do, give it your all. Whether that be Primrose, or the pop-up shop, or the Sharks. Don't skimp on your own talents."

"That's good advice."

"Good," I say, pulling into the parking lot of the restaurant. "Noelle, that concludes our business meeting."

She shoots me a surprised look and I grin.

"Now, the date can begin."

"Date?" she sputters, color high on her cheeks.

"Date," I state it clearly. I push the button that opens the car doors. "I don't take just anyone to Rinaldo's, only the people I'm trying to impress."

She recovers quickly from her surprise. Her blue eyes shimmer with a mixture of excitement, uncertainty, and curiosity. "What makes you think I'm so easily impressed?"

I laugh and shake my head. "I don't think you're easily impressed. That's why this is my starting point."

We exit the car and I take her hand, not caring that I'm not playing this cool at all. I want to feel her soft skin, I want to savor the heat of her skin as it melds with mine.

"You know, for a renowned business guy, you're showing all your cards," she remarks as a member of the staff opens the door for us.

I usher her inside and flash her a smile. "I'm too old for games, Noelle. I can be a shark, no pun intended—"

She rolls her eyes.

"In a boardroom. But in my personal life, I've always been upfront. Honest. And I'd like to take you to dinner, as my date."

Her expression softens and a sweetness that causes my heart to accelerate washes over her face. It's a hesitancy, an innocence, that I simultaneously want to keep there and erase. I give her fingers a reassuring squeeze and she applies the same pressure back.

A silent understanding passes between us. Tonight is a date, but it's more than that. It's the start of something new, something thrilling and breathtaking and a little bit forbidden.

But I'm not backing down and, from the gleam in her eyes, neither is she.

The hostess greets us and escorts us to our table. The restaurant, a small, rustic, and charming space that only locals know about opens before us. We're seated in the back right corner, my favorite table in the place. Mostly because it offers privacy but also because the views are something else.

I help Noelle out of her coat, folding her scarf into the sleeve of her parka and hanging both of our winter gear on a nearby coatrack.

When I return to the table, she gives me a breathtaking smile. "I like it here. It's…cozy."

"The food is phenomenal. And I like the vibe too," I agree. "It feels real, like you could be in someone's kitchen for a holiday meal."

"Exactly," she laughs, scrunching up her nose. "Not that I had many of those. But in college, my roommate invited me home for Thanksgiving. Dad was traveling with the team, so I agreed and it was…" she trails off, sighing.

"One of those big, loud, overbearing family holidays you see in movies."

"Yes!" Her eyes shine, her face open and brilliant. "It was perfect."

Her desire to have those things, the same things I hope for, warms my heart. "I know exactly what you mean," I murmur as our server stops at our table.

We hear the evening's specials, and after checking with Noelle that she likes red wine, I order two of my favorite bottles.

"Two," she says, surprised, after the server leaves.

"So you can try them both," I explain. I'd like to learn what taste she prefers. The softer notes of a pinot noir or the full-bodied cabernet sauvignon?

She gives me a look. "You're spoiling me, Scott."

"You deserve to be treated well, Noelle. Let me be the one to spoil you."

She sucks in a breath, and I wish I could take a photo of the surprise in her expression. The disbelief in her eyes. Jesus, who has this beautiful, intelligent, engaging woman been dating?

Vowing to spoil her every chance I can, I murmur my thanks to the server and try the first wine. Once our glasses are poured, I lift my glass to Noelle and propose a toast. "To new beginnings. To you, Noelle."

She blushes but clinks her glass against mine.

Then, we each take a tentative sip.

I make a decision. And I don't look back.

CHAPTER 7
NOELLE

T he restaurant is tucked away, a quiet venue off the beaten path of the North End. Being here with Scott feels like being wrapped in our own little world. One where he and my father aren't rivals. One where he hasn't offered me a professional opportunity that will help grow my business but anger Daddy. One where all the complications of who we are, of what's expected of us, doesn't exist.

Seated at a back table in Rinaldo's gives us the freedom and security to just be two people with an undeniable attraction. One I want to give into even though logic holds me back.

It's not the first time my heart and head haven't been on the same page, and each time I've listened to my heart—ahem, Chris comes to mind—it's come back to bite me in the ass.

But that doesn't make my heart stop hoping or my head stop wanting. I pluck a garlic knot from the basket between us and tear into the comforting carbohydrates.

Something about this causes Scott to smile, the corners of his eyes crinkling.

"Finally," he murmurs.

I quirk an eyebrow.

"I usually kill the breadbasket on my own."

I snicker. "I'm not your usual type, Scott."

This makes his grin widen. "What's my usual type?"

I tilt my head to the side, half studying him, half thinking. Over the years, I've seen Scott at galas or events, usually with a beautiful woman on his arm. But never the same woman twice.

"No strings attached," I summarize.

The curve of his mouth flattens and his eyes grow serious, the green almost glowing in the candlelight. "Go on."

"You like to keep things simple. Uncomplicated."

"Unless the reward is too great to back down from."

His words send a ripple through my chest, my heart clanging, my temples throbbing. Does he mean me? Am I a reward to keep? Or an instant gratification desire?

"You're more than worth it, Noelle," he speaks directly, as if reading my thoughts. I don't know what he reads on my expression but his eyes flare, the truth in them unmistakable. "I'd mess it all up for a chance with you."

I suck in an inhale, the sound calming to the blood rushing through my head. "Scott," I murmur, "I don't want to confuse business with—"

He shakes his head and I cut myself off. "The pop-up shop, the business stuff, that's separate. I've eaten from Primrose Sweets," he reminds me. "You're talented, Noelle, and your bakery can stand on its own, without your surname or your father's presence in New York. Look how well you're already managing in Boston."

I give a small nod in agreement.

Scott leans forward, his voice strong but quiet. Laced with a resolve, a confidence, that allows me to believe in his sincerity.

"Business is business," he repeats, his gaze sharp on my

face. "But the things I feel for you, the things I want with you…it's a whole different ballgame."

My mouth twitches at his baseball reference and he catches it, his eyes flaring with amusement.

"I'm going to make a mess of things unless you tell me not to. Unless you tell me you don't feel this between us." He gestures between us, his fingers sweeping over the breadbasket.

I clear my throat. "I'd be lying if I said that."

"I know. So give me a shot."

I laugh lightly, way out of my element here. No man has ever been so direct with me, so forthcoming and honest and unwavering in his attentions and declarations. "A shot?"

"What's holding you back from saying yes?"

I bite my bottom lip, choosing my words carefully. "Well, my dad, for one."

Scott nods, as if he expected this. "What else?"

"This life, the hockey world…" I trail off, not wanting to insult him but wanting him to understand just how much of my life it's already dictated. How much I think of a future that doesn't revolve around a hockey team, an arena, and ice.

Understanding dawns on his expression and he nods once, neatly. Accepting. "You want out."

"I don't know," I admit. "Sometimes. After, Chris and I broke up—"

Scott makes a face.

I roll my eyes. "Well, it put things into perspective for me. This world, the expectations and demands, the day-to-day challenges and inability to plan." I pause, shrugging. "It's a lot. And it doesn't really go away."

"No," he agrees. "It doesn't."

I toy with the garlic knot on my plate, breaking it into little crumbs. It's completely inappropriate for a business meeting, or a date, or dinner in general, and yet, seeing the little pieces of flaky bread lining the perimeter of my plate eases me some.

"I don't know what I want," I admit quietly. "But I know it's not a repeat of my childhood."

Scott's expression softens. "It was lonely."

"At best," I admit. "Hockey always came first. With Dad, our family, then with Chris. Nothing else ever mattered."

"It wouldn't be like that with me."

The corner of my mouth hitches. "How can you be so sure?"

"I won't lie and say hockey isn't a huge part of my life. For so long, it's been the guiding thing, the constant. But I've been lonely too, Noelle. And I want more…out of life, for myself. Just, more."

I tip my head in understanding, in acknowledgment.

"I'm just asking for a shot," he reminds me.

"But we both know nothing between us can ever be casual," I point out.

"No," he agrees, his eyes burning as they drink mine in, desperate for me to agree to what he's proposing. Sure, he's wording it in platitudes, a chance, but if what sparks between us grows just a little bit more, if I like him even more than I do right now, there will be no turning back. I won't go against Dad for a casual fling and he knows that.

He's asking me for the more he seeks. And I want to say yes.

But I don't.

I take a long sip of my wine, letting the bold flavor settle some of my thoughts, my nerves.

"I'm not sure yet what the future holds for me, Scotty."

The corner of his mouth lifts at the old nickname and he nods in understanding.

"I respect that, Noelle. But will you still give me a shot?"

At his expectant, almost hopeful expression, I smile.

"Yes," I say clearly, my heart lurching. "I'll give you a shot, Scott. But a shot isn't a guarantee."

He grins, knowing he's won, that I can't turn him away

even though I should. Even though I thought I would. "Nothing in life is a guarantee."

"Your entrees are served," our server announces, appearing at the end of our table with two dinner plates. As she lays down our entrees and explains our meals, I can't tear my eyes away from Scott.

With his salt and pepper temples and the lines that bracket his mouth, he's more experienced, more sophisticated, and more certain than I am.

At the same time, his eyes flare with a desire, a heat, I understand perfectly. Losing myself in that, I pick up my fork. *"Buon appetito."*

He grins wolfishly. "Nothing could be better than this."

I blush at the meaning behind his words and dip my head.

Adding smooth and sweet to the list of adjectives growing in my mind, I'm certain that Chris has nothing on a man like Scott. He's already built his empire, already chased his dreams, already made his fortune and reputation.

Still, he wants more. And the way his eyes linger on mine proves that it's not just my body or my name, it's *me*. Suddenly, that feels like the greatest gift, the highest praise, of all, and I dig into my pasta with a gusto I haven't felt in years.

I HAVE two glasses of wine at dinner, and while I feel capable of driving, Scott insists on driving me home and having someone deliver my SUV back to the parking garage on my behalf.

"It's too much," I tell him. "I can Uber to The Meadows tomorrow morning to grab it."

He gives me a look before turning down the street to my

condo building. When he parks in front of the main entrance, he holds out an open palm. "Keys please."

I snort. "Scott, I'm serious, this is extra." Still, I rummage through my purse until my knuckles collide with my keys. Pulling them out, I remove my car key and drop it into his hand.

"Get used to it."

I roll my eyes but his remain serious. He's not joking; he really is the kind of man who goes above and beyond, out of his way, for others. While I've witnessed glimpses of Scott's generosity before—hello, team baby shower?—I've never had this much attention, this much *thoughtfulness*, focused on me.

It's disconcerting, to be the object of Scott's unblinking stare.

"Thank you for dinner," I finally say. "It was delicious."

"I'm glad you said *yes*," he says simply. I know he means more than the pop-up shop, more than dinner. He means yes to *this*, whatever it is that's brewing between us, already expanding after just one shared meal.

"Me too," I admit.

"Come on, I'll walk you up." He hits the button that opens the car doors.

Scott wraps his arm around my lower back and we enter my condo building together. We're both quiet, lost in our own thoughts. At least, I am. My nerves flutter as I wonder if he's going to kiss me. Should I invite him in? Is it too forward if I do? Rude if I don't?

Before I can decide, the elevator arrives at my floor and we're standing in front of my door.

"Scott—" I start, turning into him.

He leans closer and I stifle my gasp by swallowing it, momentarily stopping my breath altogether. Scott smiles and reaches up to grasp one of my unruly curls. He draws it out slowly, letting the strands wrap around his finger, before letting it go. His fingertips graze my chin as he brushes a kiss over my cheek.

"Good night, Noelle."

"Good night, Scott," I manage to say before forcing myself to get my shit together so I can unlock the door to my apartment.

When I fumble the keys, he doesn't comment or laugh. He waits patiently until the door swings open and I step inside. Grasping the doorframe, I glance at him over my shoulder, a silent question in my eyes.

Scott's eyes burn into mine and it's no secret that his move, sexy in its simplicity, has left us both wanting more.

"I'll call you," he promises.

I dip my head in acknowledgment. "Good night."

He waits until I close the condo door. As soon as I do, a rush of excitement rolls through me, half wishing he kissed me good night and half relieved he didn't.

I peek behind the curtains in my living room and spot Scott's Tesla below, still parked in the horseshoe driveway. When he emerges from the building, I drop the curtain but continue to watch. Delight bursts in my chest as he slowly turns and looks up at my window. I wait until he drives off before making myself a cup of tea.

Excitement courses through my veins as I begin to come down from the natural high I've been caught up in all night. I have a new business venture, one that will shout out Primrose Sweets in Boston but also drum up some business for the New York location.

With that in mind, and needing to tell someone, both about the business opportunity but also about tonight, about Scott, I dial New York's bakery manager and my closest friend, Averie.

"Ave?" I say when she answers.

She groans. "You're not coming back, are you?"

I snort before a laugh bursts forth. I clap a hand over my

mouth, trying to settle my emotions. But I feel too…happy, to dash away my laughter.

"What's going on?" Ave asks.

"I said yes to the pop-up shop!" I squeal. "And, I had a date!"

"Ooh, I need to know everything. I'm getting wine."

I laugh and blow on my tea. "I just came home from dinner, and I can't tell if I'm tipsy from wine or—"

"*Him?*"

"Yes."

"Scott? It's Scott, right? As in the sexy Boston Hawks owner who sent you flowers? BTW, I'm really fucking sorry, but I accidently told your dad when he stopped by the bakery for a coffee. That's code for checking up on you."

"What?" I shriek.

"I know! I suck. I was just so annoyed that he didn't offer you a pop-up shop here in the city because I knew you'd say yes. And now, there's no way you're coming back."

I groan, tipping back my head. I definitely didn't want Dad to know that Scott sent me flowers.

"I'm sorry," Averie whispers.

I forgive her immediately because I know she didn't do it on purpose. My best friend is impulsive and has zero filter, which is one of the reasons why I adore her so much. In New York, I always keep my filter firmly in place, never saying anything that can cause a stir or scandal. "It's okay."

"Please tell me about your date with Scott, which I promise to not repeat to your father, ever. Even if he offers to hook me up with Devon Hardt."

"Devon's been traded," I chuckle, knowing how much Averie couldn't care less about hockey.

"Ah, damn. Missed my chance."

We both burst into laughter, the sound popping the ball of nerves, fears, and thrills that're lodged in my throat.

As I fill Averie in on everything that transpired with Scott this evening, I realize with a pang that she may be right. There's a chance I won't return to New York. But will I stay here? In Boston?

The thought circles in my mind long after Averie and I hang up, throughout my shower, and when I climb into bed.

In the morning, a delivery is outside my door. Four bottles of the two different wines we tried last night.

My eyebrows nearly fly off my face when I almost trip over them, hoping my SUV has been delivered.

Crouching down, I pluck out the notecard. In male handwriting, the same as the bouquet of flowers, I read:

Noelle —

Hope you slept well. We can enjoy these this weekend.

X, Scott

OMG. X? He signed it with a kiss?

Sealed with a kiss comes to mind and I burst out laughing, feeling like a teenager. I dress quickly for work, knowing that my SUV is parked in my spot, because clearly, Scott is a man with follow-through.

And I'm liking it a lot more than I thought I would.

CHAPTER 8
SCOTT

"You're whistling." Jayde glares at me accusingly when I pass her on my way to my office.

"Your nails are black," I comment, giving her hands a pointed look.

She huffs and sits on her hands, one eyebrow arched. "I guess 4 p.m. extended into dinner? Did she say yes?"

I smirk. "She said yes."

Jayde's glower transforms into a grin, and she hurries after me as I walk to my office. When I enter the space, I can hear her breathing behind me.

"We're not talking about this," I say, hanging up my wool coat and draping the scarf around the hanger.

"You're right; we're gossiping," she replies, perching on a chair.

"Can I get a coffee?"

She scoffs. "After I get some details."

"You're the most annoying human in my life," I grumble, taking a seat behind my desk and waking up my iMac.

"You're welcome. So…"

"So, Noelle is going to set up her cupcake pop-up for the game this weekend. Then, we'll take it from there."

Jayde lets out a shriek of excitement that is downright scary since she's rarely so showy with her emotions when it comes to business. My personal life, now that's another story.

"Why the hell are you so excited about this?" I ask, narrowing my eyes.

She tries to smooth out her expression but fails. "I'm excited for you, you giant ogre," she retorts.

I snicker.

"Now I'm going to Starbucks since you clearly don't appreciate me."

I laugh even harder.

"And I'm getting myself a venti mocha. On you."

I nod. Jayde moves toward the door.

"Hey, I told Noelle to reach out if—" I call out but she lifts her hand and waves without turning around.

"I'm on it, Reland."

When my office door closes, I lean back in my chair and beam. She said yes. Not just to the pop-up but to…this. Us. Giving this a chance between us. It's been too damn long since I've been this hopeful about a potential relationship, but Noelle is a game changer and I've known it for a long time.

Given her upbringing, she understands the challenges and pressures of my career. She also knows how to navigate the intensity of this industry. She's not going to be impressed by galas or designer gowns any more than she's going to be excited about a box seat Cup game. For the first time, it feels like I may have a shot at a true partnership. One without ulterior motives, one devoid of material expectations, one rooted in sincere feelings and mutual respect.

Maybe I'll get my own shot at a happily-ever-after. Maybe I'll find something real with Noelle, something that means more to me than hockey. The same way Scotch cherishes his growing family over his career. It's a clear choice in my book; I just want the opportunity to make it.

My phone rings and since I know Jayde is at Starbucks, I answer. "Scott Reland."

"Scott, hey. It's Noah," Scotch says. "I've patched in Jemmy—"

"Hey, Jem," I say to Scotch's father-in-law and one of the greatest hockey legends of all time.

"How are you, Scott?" Jem asks.

I'm about to reply when—

"I'm here too!" The sentence rings out gleefully, with a hint of a Scandinavian accent.

I huff out a laugh. "Torsten Hansen, where the hell you been hiding?"

"Still waiting for you to take a trip to Oslo, big guy," the defenseman shoots back.

I shake my head, missing Torsten, knowing that I'm going to miss Scotch. "What can I do for you guys?"

"We were hoping you could weigh in on some things regarding the Bolts. Buck," Scotch says.

In an instant, the conversation turns serious. They're calling about business, about something I can provide insight on. It's a big deal, buying a hockey team. A hell of a lot has changed since my drunken poker game and then afterwards, when I finally bought out the remaining owners to own the Hawks outright. The industry is more regulated now, the stakes are higher. I don't want to steer these men wrong, so I blow out a deep breath and settle in for the conversation.

"What can I help with? You guys want to meet in person?" I offer.

"Can't risk it," Scotch says. "Besides, Torsten's in Norway."

"I can hop a flight," Torst offers.

"What's going on?" I ask, trying to get a pulse on the matter at hand.

"We're hearing chatter Rick DiSanto and Tim Stubb—"

"From Pittsburgh?" I clarify.

"That's the one," Jem says. "Well, the two of them may block the sale of the Thunderbolts to us."

"Why?" I ask.

"That's what we're wanting to know," Torsten says. "Any pulse on it?"

I frown, at a loss for what to say. Why the hell would DiSanto and the new guy from Pittsburgh oppose the sale of the Bolts to the Hansen family? To Jeremiah Merrick and Noah Scotch? It doesn't make any sense.

"Nothing. But let me see what I can find out." I tip my chin up and nod my thanks to Jayde as she enters my office with a Starbucks cup. It's a Christmas one. I swear, it gets earlier and earlier each year. "I'll keep an ear to the ground."

"Any word you can toss out to help this go smoothly would be appreciated," Jem says.

"Of course," I agree, not voicing that as far as DiSanto goes, anything I say will be met with total resistance. "I'll see what I can do."

"Thanks, Scott," Noah says.

We talk for a few more minutes, celebrating the news of Noah and Indy expecting, before I disconnect the call.

Swiping up my coffee, I take a long pull, the caffeine clearing my mind. Jesus, it's only 8:42 a.m. and already, the day seems to have gotten away from me. I glance at my planner, at the small piles of lists and numbers Jayde laid out for me. But on top of all my regular work—meeting with senior management and the coaching staff, following up on new business ventures like hotels and restaurants I'm thinking of buying both here and abroad, touching base with my international connections, the charitable work I like to be involved in—I want to find out more about this situation with the Bolts. And what I can do to help.

ONCE I LOCK IN, time flies by. It's only the knock on my office door that has me looking up from my computer.

When Noelle enters, the stress building in my shoulder blades from a long day dissipates.

"Hey." I stand, walking closer to greet her. "What are you doing here?"

"Sorry." She gestures toward my desk. "I didn't mean to interrupt. It's just, it's 8 p.m. and—"

"It is?" I frown. Damn, the day really did get away from me. I started working on the Bolts deal, leaving a call for Buck, and reading through the terms of the sale as well as the language of the contract at 3 p.m. Five hours later and I'm still trying to piece it together.

Noelle tilts her head to the side, her gaze curious. "You okay?"

I nod, gesturing to the chairs. We both sit and she passes me a pastry box. I move to open it, but she reaches out, placing her hand on mine.

"It's a sample, for the Hawks cupcakes. But first, what's going on?"

I freeze, rooted in place by the concern in her gaze. She came here for business but quickly placed my well-being before any profit-driven ideas. It surprises me because...I'm usually a means to an end. Not that I don't have good friendships or solid relationships, but no woman has ever truly cared this early on about my day over theirs, my work before theirs.

Noelle narrows her gaze, worry shading them a darker blue, and I clear my throat.

"Nothing. I mean, I got caught up in this deal I'm working on for a friend. It kind of hijacked most of my day and I didn't realize the time, or how much I've fallen behind in getting things done."

She rolls her lips together. "You sure?"

"I'm sure," I say, meaning it. "I had Jayde take off after dinner and without her to pop her head in, I probably would have worked until midnight."

Noelle's eyes widen. "Do you do that a lot? Work 'til midnight?"

I chuckle but it's forced. "Here's where I'd usually quip about loving my job so much that it doesn't feel like work, but the truth is, I don't have anyone waiting for me at home so…"

"You bury yourself in it."

"Yes," I admit, hating how lame it makes me sound. But at forty-four, I don't have times for the stupid head games of my youth. I want real, lasting commitment. I won't settle for less and I also won't waste time coming to terms with that need.

"I understand that," Noelle says softly, one side of her mouth pulling upward. She laughs suddenly and shakes her head. "I can't even tell you how many designs I did." Her eyes flick down to the box between my hands. "I kept telling myself it's because I wanted this to be perfect for the pop-up shop but really…" she trails off, her cheeks pinking.

"Really what?"

"I want you to like them. To be impressed by…cupcakes." She lifts an arm and lets it fall back to her thigh. "I want my dad to be proud too."

All thoughts of the Bolts disappear as I stare at the beautiful woman before me. In so many ways, we're at different stages in our careers. She's still striving for that stamp of approval, desperate to be accepted for who she is and what she wants to create. But in other weays, we're right at the same phase of our lives, losing ourselves in work to stave off the lingering loneliness of not having a person. A partnership. Someone to go home to.

I open the pastry box and sigh, taking in the beautifully

decorated cupcakes. Some are simple, straightforward vanilla with blue icing. But others are decadent, with frosting that glitters like ice, and tiny confections that read Hawks or Boston.

"These are amazing, Noelle," I say seriously, looking up at her expectant expression. "You're amazing."

The color in her cheeks heightens. Her eyes warm with satisfaction, with gratitude, that I like the cupcakes. How could I not? I like everything about her.

"You're a hard worker," I comment.

"I bury myself in it sometimes," she admits. "Like you."

"Yeah. I get that." I shift in my chair, closing the lid on the box and placing the cupcakes on my desk. "Did you eat dinner yet?"

Noelle shakes her head, her eyes trained on mine.

"Are you hungry, beautiful?" I murmur, the term of endearment, so damn accurate but also so damn forward, slipping from my mouth.

Noelle nods slowly, her eyes never leaving mine.

"Have dinner with me?" I ask, my nerves tight just from her proximity, the scent of her perfume.

"Only if I can bring the wine," she murmurs.

I chuckle and stand. I extend my hand to Noelle, and she tucks her fingers into my palm. "Sounds good to me."

I help her into her coat and pull on mine, before escorting her out of The Meadows.

This time, we don't mention her car as we leave it behind. She doesn't stare pensively out the window on the ride. Instead, she looks at me, studying me, wondering things she's not ready to voice.

I don't push her. Instead, I drive home.

"Where are we?" Noelle's surprised as I pull onto my street, on the outskirts of the city.

"My place."

"You said—"

"Have dinner with me."

"Yes." Her brow furrows.

"I meant have dinner with me. Let me cook for you."

Her eyes widen and her mouth drops open. "You cook?"

"Only when there's someone to enjoy it with," I respond, parking in the U-shaped driveway.

I press the button to open the car doors and hurry around to help her out. "Come on, you can tell me if my Italian is good."

She lets out a shocked sound but holds my hand as I lead her up the front steps and into my home.

CHAPTER 9
NOELLE

"Your home is beautiful," I say around a huge bite of penne arrabbiata. "And your Italian isn't bad either."

He laughs. "Thanks. I wish I used the kitchen more but…I like having the option to cook when I have someone to share the meal with."

I glance around his state-of-the-art kitchen, outfitted with a Wolf range, Sub-Zero refrigerator, and twelve-foot island. "It's pretty spectacular."

Scott takes a sip of his wine, a new bottle he's introduced me to. "You ready for this weekend?"

"I am," I say, excited for the pop-up shop. "Now that I got my jitters out through baking—"

"Those cupcakes are incredible," he interrupts.

"And running off the ungodly amount of sugar I consumed—"

"You're a runner?" Scott asks.

"I feel good about this weekend."

"Good." He smiles. "You're going to be great."

"I hope so. And yes, I run."

"There's some great trails along the waterfront," he says, rattling off a couple of options.

"Thanks. I ran over there the other day. Chloe Crawford recommended a few."

"Austin's girl?" Scott sounds surprised.

"Yes, she came by the bakery the other day. Introduced herself."

"That was nice of her," Scott comments, taking a pull of his wine.

"It was," I agree. "She also may have conned me into joining a pole dancing class."

"What?" Scott sputters, choking on his wine.

I grin. "It's a thing. But you know what? Chloe didn't seem nosy or curious or anything. Just friendly and open and wanting to buy some cupcakes for Vivi, who, apparently, everyone thinks is having a girl because she's on a sweets kick."

Scott chuckles. "I heard that old wives' tale too. But, yes, the BHH women—that's what they started calling themselves —are a good group. To be honest, none of them kick up trouble or drama, which is unheard of. They're all just—"

"Nice?"

"Supportive," he explains.

"That's incredible."

"Tell me about it. When the girls are happy, the guys are more focused on the ice."

"I'd argue that that has a lot to do with the culture of your program."

Scott looks up, surprised. "What do you mean?"

I tip my head. "The culture at The Meadows, the energy, I felt it the second I entered. It's warm and inviting. The vibe is chill, encouraging. When the owner cultivates that, hires the right people who add to the vision, it trickles down. To the players, to their outlook, to their partners. It's amazing really but you've built a family, Scott."

He looks truly astounded by my words, as if he never considered this before. As if he didn't realize he wasn't building something so much greater, truer, than a hockey team. "You really think so?"

"I know so."

"Hmm," is all he says but I can tell that his mind is turning. I can tell that my words pleased him. His shoulders relax a little and I take comfort in that, in knowing that I can help settle his thoughts as easily as he's been settling mine.

"You guys are having a great season," I add.

"Yeah, well, let's hope we can keep it going. We're playing Vancouver this weekend."

"Ugh." I roll my eyes.

Scott snickers. "Not a fan?"

"The players are always rough, trying to make a point that they're badass even when their play sucks."

Now Scott is laughing. "I love that you know the teams, can talk shop. It's sexy as hell, beautiful girl."

I blush under his praise but I'm grinning back. It could be because he said the word *sexy*, or because he's called me beautiful again, or because I'm on my third glass of wine, but suddenly, I don't want this night to end. I want to stay right at Scott's table and talk to him until the sun comes up.

"What are you thinking about?" he calls me out, his tone more curious than teasing.

"You."

"What about me?" He places his fork down.

"I like this, with you, more than I thought I would."

"You're going to have to decipher that one for me."

I snort. "I swore to myself that moving to Boston was going to be good for me."

He rears back. "Hasn't it been?"

"Yes," I say quickly, to reassure him. "But I wanted the distance from the city to also gain distance from hockey. And now, with you, I'm right back in the center of it all."

"And?"

"And I didn't expect to enjoy it this much. Being with you,

it's different. Your hockey outlook isn't the same as my dad's—"

"I should hope not," he grumbles.

I keep going, "Or Chris's."

"I can't believe you used to date Chris Rickson."

I shrug.

"What happened between you guys anyway?" His tone holds more than just curiosity.

"He was all hockey, all the time. And I...I wanted something else."

Scott purses his lips, considering my words. "I'm hockey all the time too, babe."

"But it's different," I retort, unable to explain exactly how it's different. Maybe it's too early to tell. But so far, Scott's surprised me in the best ways possible. As much as I shouldn't feel this way about him, I can't halt my feelings. I can't turn them off. "You're different, Scott."

"So are you, Noelle."

"I've never been in the hockey world before and felt so... at ease."

"I'm glad I can make you feel that way," he answers seriously. "I just want what's best for you, babe."

"And I want what's best for you."

"Good." Scott smiles. "Then let's have some of these cupcakes, yeah?"

I groan as he produces the cupcake box I brought to his office earlier.

"I'd offer you a coffee but I have no idea how to work the machine. You'll have to ask Claire Merrick. Or Jayde." He places the cupcakes on plates.

I laugh and walk over to the fancy contraption. "Working at a bakery has taught me a few things."

Scott chuckles. While he brings the cupcakes to the table, I fiddle with the expresso machine and make us two lattes.

Bringing them over, I slip into the chair beside his, when earlier we were sitting across from each other.

Scott takes note and places a cupcake on my plate. Then, his hand finds my thigh under the table and rests there. He takes a big bite of cupcake and groans as the sweetness fills his mouth. "These are so fucking good."

I grin, taking a nibble of mine. "I'm glad you think so."

He glances over at me. "I'm not kidding, Noelle. You're something else."

"So are you, Scotty."

Cupcakes and coffee drags on as Scott and I fall into easy conversation about the topic I usually try to avoid, hockey. But with him, it's not heated or negative, it's exciting and refreshing. He tells me about upcoming players, about ways the league can change to be more inclusive, more socially responsible, about the steps the Hawks are taking to initiate sparks of that change. As I listen to him speak, I'm filled with the same energy and excitement I feel when baking something new in the kitchen.

Scott is inspiring and I revel under his attention, wanting to make this moment between us last.

"It's late," he murmurs when the grandfather clock in his living room strikes midnight, chiming.

"I should get going." I push back my chair and move to stand. "I'll call an Uber."

Scott's hand settles on top of mine, rooting me in place. His eyes are piercing when they meet mine. "Stay, beautiful. I want you to stay."

I suck in an inhale, rolling my lips together. I know what he's asking me. And fuck, I want to say yes. Yes!

Scott tips his head. "You can take my room. I'll sleep in the guest room or—"

"Yes," I blurt it out before I lose my nerve. "But I want to take your room with you in it." I'm proud when my tone doesn't waver. Because while I'm sure as hell nervous, completely blurring the line of business and pleasure, I don't want to look back.

I want to share tonight with Scott. I want to stay. I want to say a thousand times, yes.

MASCULINE and strong come to mind when I enter Scott's bedroom. The space is impeccably clean, uncluttered, and organized. A dark gray accent wall offsets the black of his bedframe. A soft rug meets my toes as I walk farther into the space, spinning around to take in the big screen television, the wood paneling behind it, and the fireplace in one corner. His room is contemporary in style but warm and inviting in feel, like his office. I grin when I realize just how much of himself Scott poured into the Hawks offices. I run my hand over the linen bedsheets, already desperate to slip between them.

"I like your room," I comment, turning and flashing him a sassy smirk.

"I like you in it," he replies, stepping closer to me. His fingers play over my hair, tugging on my riotous curls. "Wanna see this blonde hair all over my pillows." He drops his head and presses a single kiss against the side of my neck.

I shiver from the contact and Scott pulls back, slipping the thin strap of my camisole off my shoulder. He moves slowly, languidly, as if we have all the time in the world. And I suppose we do.

Used to the rush and tumble of men from bars, or Chris, this feels different. More mature, more certain.

My abdomen tightens at the thought. Am I really doing this with Scott? This is a big step for two people who will always be in the same circle, for two people who will have to combat a lot of scrutiny if our connection goes public.

Not to mention, a hell of a lot for a girl who swore she didn't want this life. Didn't want this future.

Scott tilts his head. "What are you thinking about?"

"Everything," I murmur, surprised by my own honesty. I was never this forthcoming with Chris, preferring to smooth things over with our mouths and fingers than with words.

Scott's hand settles on my hip. "Talk to me, beautiful. I want your thoughts as much as I want this body."

"This changes things," I begin, trying to sort out my thoughts before I say something I'll regret. I just don't know if in the long run, that will be continuing tonight with Scott. Or, in the short run, ruining everything between us.

God, what is wrong with me? This is *Scotty*. While his attention confused me at first, he's been nothing but patient, understanding, caring, since we started talking.

"I-I like you, Scott," I blurt out.

He smirks. "I think it's obvious how I feel about you, Noelle."

"I just, I don't know, I'm not sure—"

"If you can make the big commitment?" he guesses, simplifying the thoughts whirling in my head.

"It's not the commitment to you so much as the commitment to hockey," I say, feeling foolish. Since Chris, I've resisted the dating pool of professional athletes and men connected to the sports industry. But I don't want to resist Scott and it both entices and worries me. When I'm with him, it's like I'm under his spell, caught up in the moment. But when I think about us, logically, it seems like our relationship will be a constant uphill battle, wrought with sacrifices I always said I wouldn't make.

But given how new this thing between us is, aren't I over-analyzing it?

Scott hooks a finger under my chin and lifts my head until my eyes meet his understanding gaze. Gah.

"This doesn't have to be a forever, beautiful. I just don't

want it to be a one-night only. Explore what's between us with me, be here for it. I know this is complicated. I know this isn't what you expected. Hell, I didn't expect it either. If you don't want to give this a shot, tell me now. No hard feelings. We keep our relationship strictly platonic with some business tossed in. But if you can give me a chance, a real one, then let me prove to you that hockey doesn't define our future. Or our relationship. Only you and me can do that, Noelle."

I let out a slow exhale, noting the truth in his gaze. I'd be an idiot to turn down a man like Scott just because I can't figure my own shit out. And I may be indecisive about my future with hockey, but I'm not dumb. Not when a man as incredibly kind, considerate, and attentive as Scott is standing in front of me, words dripping with sincerity, eyes brimming with promise.

I lift my chin farther, brushing my mouth over his. This time, our kiss holds an edge, the frenetic need to prove the intent of our words. We're giving this a shot. A real chance. With more between us than the moment. More than tonight.

Scott Reland is one of the sexiest men I've ever seen. When I unbutton his dress shirt and the material parts, his abs are a thing of folklore. Tipsy off wine, high on him and his words, a shiver works up my spine.

Scott clasps my wrists, adding pressure until I meet his gaze.

"We don't have to do *this* tonight, Noelle. I don't want to rush with you. I want…" He sighs, a puff of laughter mixed with disbelief. "With you, I want to slow down. I want you to be sure."

His words send an undercurrent through my veins, tugging me, all of me, closer to him. His hands release my wrists to rest on my shoulders, palms sliding up and down my arms. "I want to know you."

"You're getting there." As I say the words, I realize how true they are. In a handful of weeks, Scott has taken more time to truly know me, to understand my motivations, my thoughts, my outlook, than any man in the last handful of years. More than most of my friendships too, save Averie. "But I want this. Tonight." I say it like a declaration, the truth shimmering in the space between us. My issues with hockey have to do with the future I envision for myself. But not with Scott. No, when I look up at him, I lose myself in the fire that flares in his green eyes.

Content with my verbal reassurance, Scott dips his head. His lips find mine as his hands trail over my body, one palm centering in the middle of my back, the other hooking around my hip. His cologne washes over me like mountain air and I tremble in his arms, already feeling my body tighten and coil, shiver and shake.

My hands latch onto his shoulders as I move up onto my tippy toes, eagerly meeting his kiss with my own. When Scott hauls me closer, pulling my body into his strong frame, I go willingly. I close my eyes, surrender my body, and lean into him, giving everything between us a chance to blossom.

CHAPTER 10
SCOTT

Noelle tastes like fresh snow, pure and pristine. Her skin is like silk against my lips, her hair, an angel's halo, a shock of gold against my dark bedsheets, as I lay her out in the center of my bed.

She pushes my shirt off my shoulders, and I shake it to the floor, standing briefly to drop my dress pants and tug off my socks. When I'm dressed in nothing but black briefs, her eyes widen, drinking in my body with the appreciation of an art connoisseur. Her perusal quickens my pulse, causing my cock to stir, eager and needy to be inside of her.

But no matter what I need, hers will always come first. And tonight, I want to savor everything she's offering, worship her body for the treasure it is. I bend forward and pop the button on her dark jeans, so tight, they're like a second skin. I peel them off, rolling them over her hips, and tugging them off her long legs. A scrap of lace covers the V between her thighs, and I nearly growl when I see it, a deep purple that causes the creaminess of her thighs to glow. I snake my way up her body, pressing kisses and nips along the tantalizing slope of her torso. Her long legs tangle with mine as I pay extra attention to the swell of her breasts, before tugging the silky camisole over her head. Her bra, another lacy number in the same shade of purple, barely conceals her pert nipples. I roll one tight nub between my fingers as Noelle gasps, her eyes flying to mine.

I smirk at her, my cock twitching against her thigh as lust colors her sapphire eyes. Never breaking eye contact, I drag down the cup of her bra, my fingertips softly drifting over her peachy pink nipple, before circling the outer edge. Her eyes continue to darken, her breathing hitching. Involuntarily, her knees fall open and I settle more firmly between her thighs. I give her other nipple the same attention before dropping my head and sucking the hard nub into my mouth, lightly grazing it with my teeth.

Noelle gasps, the sounds falling from her mouth, sweet and needy, turning me on. That, and the slickness between her legs as I drag my fingers over the lace, feeling her need seep out between the delicate pattern. She moans once, her hands reaching for me. One grasps the back of my head, her fingernails grazing against my scalp while the other wraps around my bicep, squeezing.

I know exactly what she wants and, Christ, I want to be the man to give it to her. I tug her thong to one side and dip my fingers into her channel, dragging the pads of my fingertips over her folds, moving her heat over the nub of her clit.

She pulls my head down and I kiss her hard, the heat of her mouth melding with her heat on my fingers. I tease her for a few seconds before finding a pace she seems to like. Her breathing picks up and she begins to grind against my hand, needy for my touch, needy for me.

Fuck, it's a heady feeling. It's exhilarating, watching a woman like Noelle, strong, successful, sexy, break apart under my touch. But she does, on a cry that has her back arching, her breasts pressing into my chest.

"Oh my God. Scotty. I swear, I don't, I'm not—" she

murmurs, trying to make sense of everything that just happened.

"Shh," I hush her, slipping down her body, the scent of her like a siren, calling me to the space between her thighs. "Let me taste you, beautiful." I drag my tongue through her sensitive folds and she bucks, reaching for me.

"No, no, it's your turn. Let me, I—"

I swat away her hand, wanting to make this so fucking good for her that she gives me the chance I want. A chance at forever. There will be plenty of time for me to sink inside of her but right now, I want to watch her break apart again. I want to see how many times I can make her come for me tonight. I bury my head between her thighs, lapping at her need as her body tightens once more. Dipping two fingers into her channel, I pump slowly while my mouth kisses her hard. In another instant, she shatters again, swearing loudly.

I chuckle at the profanities that fall from her luscious lips.

"Christ, you are sexy," I tell her truthfully, swiping my fingers over my lips.

"Get over here," she demands, bossy.

I grin and move up her body until her hands clutch my shoulders.

"Get on your back," she says.

I lift an eyebrow, surprised by the authority in her tone.

"Please," she adds.

I snort but turn onto my back. I'm pitching one hell of a tent, my cock rock fucking hard and desperate for her to touch me, suck me, ride me, hell, do whatever the fuck she wants with me.

Noelle presses a quick kiss to my lips before pulling my briefs off my body and tossing them to the floor.

"Jesus," she whispers, her eyes darting over my body as her hand grips my shaft and slowly begins to pump. "You're fucking sexy, Scott," she tosses my words back at me. Then, she swings a leg over my hips until she's straddling me. The visual of her dragging the tip of my cock through her folds has me straining and swearing.

Noelle just smirks, as if it's her turn to torture me. Fuck, I guess it is.

But then she sinks down on top of me and all thoughts cease to exist. Instead, I'm enraptured. Noelle begins to move, taking me completely, grinding against me, making me see fucking stars.

Her curls frame her face, a few sweaty strands sticking to her neck, as she works me over. Her mouth parts, plump lips I want to bite, but her eyes, her eyes hold mine with a want that makes me feel like a fucking king. A deity.

"Fuck, Scott," she murmurs, increasing the pace. One of her palms slaps down in the center of my chest and I flinch from the sting, welcoming the thin line of pain and pleasure.

I grip her hips, digging my fingers into her flesh, as she moves faster. She works me into a frenzy, one where I can't recall my name, but I sure as fuck remember hers. "Noelle," I holler it once before I come hard inside of her, growling as I watch my semen drip down her thighs. "Fuck, beautiful." I pull her toward me and kiss her hard. I turn her in my arms until we're lying side by side, me still inside of her, my seed staining both of our skin. "We didn't use a condom. I, Jesus, I forgot," I mutter, stunned. I don't think I've ever forgotten in forty-four years. Except when I was seriously committed to a woman and we had the talk, got tested, and did all the things in the right order. But never on a first night. Never—

"I'm clean. And I have an IUD," Noelle says easily.

I frown. "I'm clean too, baby. But we should have talked about it."

She smiles, a sated glow on her cheeks. "I got caught up in the moment."

I snort, kissing the tip of her nose. "Yeah, me too. But still…"

"It's okay," she says, meaning it, before a yawn takes over. "I, you, this was a good night, Scotty."

"This was the fucking best, Noelle," I agree, pulling her tighter against my chest. I drop my hand onto the center of her belly, watching as her eyelids grow heavy. "We need to clean up."

She nods, her cheek rubbing against my bicep, but she doesn't move.

I chuckle and brush her hair away from her face, memorizing the pinky glow of her skin. Then, I slip out of her, move to the side of the bed, and swing her up into my arms.

"What are you doing?" She laughs, clutching at me.

"Taking you to the shower. With me." I grin, entering my bathroom.

"Damn," she mutters as she takes in the space. My shower is huge, with a built-in bench, water jets, and a massive rain showerhead. I sit Noelle down on the bench while I turn on the water and adjust the temperature. When it's hot and steamy, I tug her underneath, wrap her in my arms, and kiss her hard.

"What's that for?" she asks, grinning up at me.

"Go away with me," I reply.

Her eyes widen and a surprised chuckle bursts from her mouth. "What?"

"Go away with me," I repeat.

"Now? You're a month into the season and—"

"Two weeks. Me and you, one night. New Orleans. I want to take you to my city."

She lifts her eyebrows. "Boston's not your city?"

I smirk, tipping my head toward hers. New Orleans is the home of my heart, and I don't share it freely, but I want to take Noelle. Show her the places I love, show her the home I made there. "It is. I love Boston. But New Orleans... I went my first time in high school and something about it captured me. I go every year, around this time; I even have a place there. It's my home in a way. The city that makes me feel most…alive. And I want to *feel* it with you. Play hooky with me, beautiful." I press because I want her to say yes. I want to take her to my someplace special and enjoy watching her eyes dance and her face light up. I want to lavish her with every surprise, give her every damn thing she desires.

She looks at me, her expression incredulous before she bursts into disbelieving laughter. She tips her head up, her curls getting doused in water that straightens them halfway down her back. My hands grip the edges and tug.

"Yes," she agrees. "I'd love to see New Orleans with you."

"Okay," I say, kissing her hard as the water pelts us from above.

Before we can wash, I take her again. This time, she's splayed against the glass of my shower, imprinting her body in a sexy fucking portrait on the steamy shower door. It's a visual I won't forget for as long as I live.

With a woman I want for all my days.

CHAPTER 11

NOELLE

"New Orleans!" Averie shrieks.

"Shh!" I hush, more a reflex than anything. "It's only for a night."

"Girl, if I'm dragging my ass to Boston, you better go for at least two," she says, making me laugh.

"So, you'll come?" The thought of leaving town and entrusting my bakery to my two new employees was a hard cookie to swallow. I thought of every possible thing that could go wrong and almost told Scott I can't go.

But, not wanting to disappoint him, I called Averie and…

"Yes, I'll come," my best friend agrees.

"Yes!" Now I'm the one shrieking and Averie is telling me to quiet down.

"Next Wednesday?" she asks.

"Yes. It's only for one night," I reiterate. "Scott has to be back for Friday's game, and I can't leave the bakery for that long. Besides, you can stay the weekend. Help me run my new pop-up shop. I'm trialing things out at the game this Saturday so in two weekends, I'll be an old pro."

Averie laughs. "You sure you're okay with me leaving Primrose New York for like five days? Because I haven't taken a vacation in two years and Boston isn't anywhere near the top of my list."

"See if Jay can cover. You know what, I'll call him. And shut it. Seeing me should be at the top of your list. If you stay the weekend, we can hang out. And… you can meet him."

"Damn," my bestie murmurs. "You want me to meet him? This is serious, Noelle. I can't remember the last time you wanted me to meet a guy."

"Scott's different," I say, somewhat defensively.

"I didn't mean it like that," Averie laughs, seeing right through me. "I'm happy for you, babe. Did you tell Papa DiSanto yet?"

"Yes," I grumble, recalling that awful conversation.

"Babe, you're hitting your mid-thirties, it's okay to not have your father's approval for every decision you make."

"I know," I sigh, rubbing my forehead. While logically, I know Averie is right, I can't ease the guilt that spins in my chest for causing Dad's disappointment. I hate knowing that Mom would be disappointed too.

Averie sighs. "Well, I'm in. I can't wait to see you, check out Primrose 2.0, and meet the man that's got my girl fucking swooning."

I don't even deny it because, it's true.

"Damn," Averie laughs. "Okay, I gotta go. I'm going to scare the shit out of Jay to make sure he can handle things next week without me."

I laugh, feeling badly for Averie's second in command at the New York bakery. "I can't wait to see you. And thank you."

"Me too. 'Bye babe."

I hang up feeling much better about heading out of town in two weeks. I open my messages with Scott and respond to his last text.

NOELLE

Averie's coming to run the bakery. New
Orleans is a go!

SCOTT

Good. See you tonight, beautiful.

I smile at his text, already counting down the hours until I can get back in his bed.

"Who's the guy?" A female giggle pulls me from my thoughts, and I look up, blushing when I spot Chloe, Indy, and Vivi on the other side of the counter.

I shake my head, laughing with them, as I slip my phone into my back pocket. "What can I get you girls?"

Chloe lifts an eyebrow but doesn't say anything.

Instead, Indy laughs. "Slick, Ms. DiSanto."

Vivi rolls her eyes. "I need an eclair. I swear, I'm gaining double the recommended weight, but I just want sweets. Like, all the time. And my husband is too damn good to deny me."

"In anything," Chloe says pointedly, lifting an eyebrow in my direction.

I laugh with them and fix a plate of sweets and some coffees. Since it's the afternoon lull and the bakery is empty, I join them at the table with my own latte.

"How are you feeling? When are you due?" I ask Genevieve.

"Not 'til March," she sighs, biting into an eclair.

"Expect us to be regulars," Chloe adds.

"I'd love that," I say, meaning it more than just having the added business. I like the BHH girls, and I'd love to get to know them better.

"I hear you're opening a pop-up shop at the arena this weekend," Indy says.

"I am," I say cautiously, not sure how much information to give away.

"That's awesome," Chloe says sincerely. "I know things

are still new for you here so if you need help with anything..." she trails off, gesturing between her and Indy.

"We'd love to help," Indy adds.

My hesitancy disappears and I see what Scott meant about these women being drama free and supportive. "That's very generous of you both. But don't you want to watch the game?"

Indy shrugs. "Noah's not playing. To be honest, I'd rather eat cupcakes and have girl talk."

Vivi snickers, polishing off her eclair. "Same. But don't tell Dec I said that."

"Well, if you're sure...I mean, I'd love the company if you want to pop by," I say slowly, not wanting to put them to work but not wanting to turn down their help either.

"Done!" Chloe declares. "It will be fun. Claire and Abbi will be around too. I know Bella would love to help, but she'll have her hands full with the twins."

Indy nods and continues to fill me in on The Who's Who and The Who's with Who of the Hawks. My head begins to swirl with the names and information. Vivi, seeing my expression, reaches over and pats my hand.

"Don't worry," she says in her soft Tennessee drawl, "you'll get used to it."

Indy nods, shooting me a knowing look.

I smile back, tilting my head to the side as I try to understand the intent behind their words and looks. Do they know about Scott and me?

Indy shakes her head and places a hand on her stomach. Then she sighs and pulls out her phone. "Sorry, girls, I need to head out. I'll see you this weekend, Noelle."

"Sure." I stand as the others offer to walk out with her.

"Thank you for these," Vivi says, wrapping me in a one-armed hug as I press a box with eclairs into her hands. "You have the best eclairs in the city," she whispers.

I chuckle, nodding my thanks, as the girls leave as quickly as they arrived.

Once they're gone and the bakery is quiet once more, I pull my phone out. A missed call from Dad mocks me, and I know we need to have another conversation about the pop-up shop.

But can't it wait until after my night with Scott? I just want to stay wrapped up in this happy bubble a little while longer.

"THESE ARE INCREDIBLE," a woman mumbles to her friend, cupcake sticking to the corners of her mouth. She looks at me. "You're a unicorn."

I laugh, thanking her and pushing a cupcake toward her friend, a skeptical-looking woman.

"Try it," the first woman demands, nodding enthusiastically. "It's worth another hour on your Peloton."

The second woman huffs but takes a small bite before moaning so appreciatively, several men nearby look over.

I stifle another laugh, happily ringing up another half dozen order.

"Damn, this is fire," Abbi Walsh, badass girlfriend to the Hawks goalie, Luca Pandatelli, comments, coming up beside me. She pushes up the sleeves on her Hawks hoodie. "Tell me how I can help."

I shoot her a grateful glance and direct her to the line of waiting customers. For the next twenty minutes, until the face-off, Abbi and I are hustling. The cupcakes are flying from the display case I made, and I start to worry that we won't have any treats left for intermission.

Which, all things considered, is a freaking awesome issue to have.

"Whew," Abbi says after cashing out the last customer. "That was intense."

"Tell me about it," I agree, glancing at the slim pickings left over. "I didn't expect that to happen. At all."

Abbi grins. "Feels good though, doesn't it? To know that people truly love your cupcakes."

"Yeah," I agree, grinning back at her. "Feels amazing. I wish my dad…" I trail off, surprised that I even brought that sentiment up. But I wish Dad could see me, could see *this*, and realize how successful my bakeries can be. How well they *are* doing. I wish he could admit that this isn't just a phase but my passion, the business I want to build instead of the one I'm supposed to inherit.

Abbi sighs. "Girl, I've got bigger daddy issues than all the women in our crew combined."

I laugh at her statement but at the pain that wells in her eyes, I realize she's speaking from a place of hurt. I reach over to squeeze her hand before passing her a cupcake.

She snorts but takes a huge bite. "You must really like me if you're passing over your product like this. You've got less than a dozen left."

"Yeah," I say, thinking about how I can get more cupcakes to the arena in time for the intermission rush. I can call Merry, who is currently running the show, and have an Uber driver rush them over? I laugh at my own brilliant problem-solving when a breathless voice reaches my ears. I turn and my mouth drops open.

"I'm here!" Chloe announces, several large bags swinging from her arms.

"No Starbucks?" Abbi asks.

Chloe shoots her a death glare and Abbi chuckles, slipping in front of the pop-up shop to help her with the bags.

"What's going on?" I ask, springing into action when I realize the bags are filled with cupcake boxes from Primrose.

"I messaged her," Abbi says casually, like she didn't just

problem solve a 'hell of a lot faster, and more efficiently than me.

"And I ran by the bakery. Your new girl, Merry, helped me out, and voila!" Chloe flares her arm out in front of the display case that Abbi is neatly restocking. "Merry's going to push your eclairs and mille-feuille today. I tried both and don't think she'll have a hard time."

Abbi laughs but I'm still standing there in disbelief.

"Wow, you guys, thank you." My tone is heavy on the sincerity and both girls turn to look at me.

"It's kind of our thing," Abbi explains.

I frown, confused.

"Helping each other out," Chloe explains. "God knows it isn't easy being in a relationship with an NHL player. A lot of your dreams or goals get sidelined by accident, or necessity, and the extra support isn't always readily available."

"Unless you make it so," Abbi tacks on, gesturing between her and Chloe. "I never would have held nearly as many outreach events this year without the girls showing up to man tables or haul around gear."

"And I definitely wouldn't be able to travel as much as I do without Abbi or Claire or one of the girls popping by to check on my Mimi, especially now that my parents are retired and split their time between here and Texas." Chloe shrugs. "We're a family."

"Yeah, but, I'm, I'm not—" I try to form a sentence. I try to explain that I'm an outsider, will always be an outsider, a Shark, without offending them. But before I can articulate this point, Abbi cuts me off.

"Please, you're one of us. We see how Scott looks at you."

I blush and close my mouth.

Chloe laughs and points at me. "Guilty."

At their genuinely curious and not at all judgy expressions, I smile. Chloe and Abbi begin to laugh, and I join in.

"This is madness," I decide, bumping Abbi out of the way to finish the cupcake display.

"Your badass business, selling out The Meadows, or having heart eyes for Scott?" Chloe asks.

"All of it," I state, unsure where to start. "When I decided to come to Boston, to open a second location, I never expected any of, this—" I flail my arm wide to encompass The Meadows, the hockey game unfolding so close, I can taste the energy of the crowd, and the man keeping it all together. Scotty.

"None of us did," Abbi quips.

Chloe nods and smiles.

"Hey! Get back to work," a friendly voice calls out.

The three of us turn and my breath catches in my throat. Scott walks toward me, oozing with confidence, the sexy kind that borders on swagger. He's dressed in dark wash jeans, a white button-down shirt, and a blue blazer. The look straddles classy and casual, as he's rocking old school Jordan's. I smile when I spot his sneakers because they're so him. An anomaly.

Abbi plates him a cupcake and passes it over. "These are delicious."

"Oh, I know," Scott says, taking a bite. A tiny bit of blue frosting dots the end of his nose and Chloe grins, rubbing at her own nose until he takes the hint. Chuckling, he adds, "My trainer is not pleased with my new cupcake addiction."

"Yeah, Scott, we all feel really bad for you. You should run more." Abbi rolls her eyes since Scott is in incredible shape. Incredible shape I have intimate knowledge of; I blush at the thought.

The rest of us laugh. Scott peeks at the full display case and frowns. "How's it been going?"

"Great!" I gush, smiling so hard my cheeks ache.

"This is round two," Abbi explains.

"We pretty much ran out and Chloe brought reinforce-ments," I tack on.

At the news, Scott flashes me a genuine smile. "It must be the Hawks colors," he jokes.

I scrunch my nose at him, and his smile widens. He gives me a quick wink and I hear Chloe's audible inhale.

"Okay, well, let me know if you girls need anything. You got this, Noelle." Scott taps my hip with his palm before waving to a man waiting for him at the end of the hallway.

"You're totally one of us," Chloe remarks.

The three of us look at each other before bursting into laughter again.

But I don't refute the claim because, what if I can be one of the Hawks girls?

CHAPTER 12
SCOTT

"You gotta come, Scott." Scotch smacks me on the back.

I chuckle and shake my head, having begged off team outings to Taps before. It never seemed right, after the occasional quick beer, to hang with the guys when I'm sure they want to blow off steam. Without me around.

"Tonight was great. Did you feel the energy? The team is gelling, Lawrence is killing it out there at right wing, Panda had some great saves..." Scotch widens his eyes at me, the dark brown blown with excitement.

I smile at one of my cornerstone players. "You're gonna make one hell of a coach, Scotch."

His eyes dart around, ensuring no one overheard him, but then he flashes me a huge grin and I know he's excited for this next chapter. Happy and motivated when most guys I know would be gutted and dragging their feet, wondering what the hell is supposed to come after hockey.

What does come after hockey? For as long as I can remember, it's the only thing I thought about. The only thing that made sense and now...

Noelle walking my way, her blonde ringlets haphazard around her face, her eyes narrowed and scanning each player she passes as if looking for someone—*God, I hope me*—dashes away thoughts of hockey. A realization slams into me so powerfully that I falter back a half step.

Her. This.

The thing that's supposed to come after hockey is…life. Beautiful, wondrous, messy, complicated life. Noelle.

"Oh, there you are." She places a hand on Noah's arm, and I straighten.

Scotch swings his gaze toward Noelle, his eyebrows drawn together.

"Indy's in the bathroom down the hall. She's really unwell," Noelle murmurs, her eyebrows doing this jumping movement that clues Scotch in. Her not-so-morning morning sickness is at it again.

"Shit. Thanks," Scotch murmurs. He turns and points at me. "Come." He glances at Noelle, his index finger now in her direction. "You too. For me, Scott."

Then he's dashing off toward the bathroom and his pregnant woman, and I'm studying the woman who is shifting all my priorities around. Even if she doesn't know it yet.

"Come to Taps," I tell her.

She scrunches her nose and slips her hands in the back pockets of her jeans, exactly the way I want to cup her ass. "Won't it be weird?"

"Why?"

"Won't people wonder?"

I shrug. "Does it matter?" I thought we agreed we were going to give this a shot. Not that we have to make a formal announcement or anything, but do we have to hide it?

Noelle glances around the space, the players hugging their families, sitting their kids on top of their shoulders. Their wives and girlfriends laughing together, taking photos, and making plans.

Her eyes cut back to mine, and she smiles. "No, it doesn't. Let's go to Taps."

"All right," I agree, wrapping my arm around her waist. I steer Noelle away from the team and toward the parking lot. "How'd you close out the stand?"

She sighs, a big whoosh of breath filled with relief, tinged with happiness. "It was amazing, Scott. I sold out. Like, there were two cupcakes left that I gave to one of the cleaners. That's it. And, as you know, we had to restock before the first intermission."

I hold her closer and her arm slips around my waist, her fingers toying with the belt loop on my pants. "I'm proud of you, Noelle." I press a kiss to the crown of her head, her curls tickling my upper lip. "You did a phenomenal job."

She pulls back to meet my gaze. "Thanks to you."

"No." I shake my head. "Don't do that. All your success is because of your hard work. You earned this, you made it happen."

Skepticism still rings her irises and I raise a questioning eyebrow.

"I guess," she mutters, snuggling deeper into my side. "Sometimes it feels like I'm wanting to be successful just to prove to my dad that I can. That I can make this work."

"So?"

"So?" She stops walking and looks up at me.

"Use it. Your wanting to prove him, others, maybe even yourself, wrong is fuel. Let that feeling, that desire to come out on top, burn. Let it propel you forward. You don't get anywhere by listening to doubters. You just move backward. Do you want to manage a hockey team or a baking empire?"

Noelle presses her lips together, trying not to laugh. "Baking."

"Then keep doing you, Noelle. It doesn't matter what anyone else thinks but if it bothers you, then let it motivate, not detract, from what you're working toward."

She nods and we begin to walk toward the car again.

"I'm glad I'm here, Scott."

"Me too, baby." I kiss her again, pretending not to see the knowing glances some of the staff are giving each other when they see Noelle and me.

But it doesn't matter. For years, hockey dictated everything; it ruled my entire life.

Right now, I don't want that. I just want the woman slipping her hand into mine, lacing our fingers, and pressing our palms together. I want to belong to a different type of team. A new family.

One that I'm making for me.

TAPS IS EXACTLY as I remember it. It's been a few seasons since I walked through the doors, but the neon signs lining the walls, the scuffed floorboards, and everyone's favorite bartender, Pete, are all the same.

"There he is!" Pete calls out, saluting me.

I lift a hand in greeting as Noelle snickers beside me. "You're quite popular," she comments, after the fourth patron stops to congratulate me on tonight's win.

"Only in Boston," I reassure her. "It's nothing like being popular in New York."

She rolls her eyes but her cheeks are rosy, her expression open and happy. Tonight, I want to fall into that with her. I want to enjoy being with my team, with my girl, and having a slice of the life I always dreamed of.

"Shots!" Pandatelli calls out as we near the bar. He points at me, a goofy grin splitting his face. "You're in, Reland. You and Ms. DiSanto."

"What is it with you and calling the girls by their last names?" Theo mutters.

Panda shrugs. "It pisses you guys off."

"You're like a toddler," Easton tells him.

Panda's grin grows, and Abbi mutters something under her breath that makes him laugh. He gestures toward Pete. "Line 'em up, my man."

"You got it, Panda." Pete shakes up some chilled Patron.

"Come on." Noelle pulls me closer into the huddle of players and their women by the bar.

Chloe and Claire immediately make room for Noelle to stand in between them, and I step up behind her, my hand on her hip. Vivi turns in her barstool and gives me a warm smile. We're both swallowed up by the huddle, welcomed and brought into the inner circle I've always felt on the outskirts of. I *should* be on the outskirts of.

But suddenly, with Noelle here, it feels different. The vibe is easygoing, and I feel like I belong.

Noelle presses a shot glass into my hand and gives me a wink.

Panda lifts his glass. "To the Hawks, more family than team, more wins than losses, let's get it this season."

A cheer rings out as all the shots glasses are thrust forward, clinking together, tequila dribbling over our wrists.

Noelle is laughing, her eyes bright and happy. She settles back against me, her hips perfectly notched in between mine. We toss back our shots and as the tequila warms my stomach, the sight of my girl interacting with my team warms my heart.

After the initial shot, I grab a round of drinks for the team and settle into conversations, moving around the bar space to catch up with players and their families.

"Good to see you out, Scott," James Ryan, one of my starting defensemen says.

"You too, James." I clasp his shoulder. After losing his wife to cancer and becoming a single dad, it's heartwarming to see him smile again. His girl Bella is a beautiful, down-to-earth, and considerate woman. Her love has helped heal the hurts that nearly broke James. It's good to see him happy again.

In fact, as I glance around the space, I realize that most of my players are thriving. They're happy, they're fulfilled, their lives are balanced.

Work and life and love.

They all have what I've been clamoring for and now, with Noelle, I finally have my shot.

My girl sidles up beside me and gives me a grin. Her eyes are a tad bit glazed, and internally I groan. "How many shots did Panda feed you?"

She giggles, bumping her hip against mine.

"That many," I guess, shooting Panda a look that he meets with a chuckle and a shrug.

I wrap my arm around Noelle. "You having fun, baby?"

"The best," she says.

"Good." I can't even be mad at Panda when Noelle is having such a good time. It's clear that she feels comfortable around the BHH girls, the team, the whole environment. She's been busting her ass, working long hours, strategizing new marketing plans. If anyone deserves a night to let loose and have some fun, it's her.

So I sit back, enjoy the scene unfolding around me, and watch the woman I have feelings for mesmerize every person she meets. A pride I've never known fills me up, rooting me to this moment.

Noelle DiSanto is it for me. I know it as surely as I know that this season, this team, this group of men, will always be more like my family than just players.

And that after this season, everything will change. Whether it's for the better or worse is up to me and my perspective.

But I also know that I'm choosing Noelle no matter what.

CHAPTER 13

NOELLE

A thrill shoots down my spine when Scott's palm anchors in the center of my back. Is it supposed to feel this way? The zip of excitement and rush of shivers from just his proximity, the scent of his cologne, the knowing that he's standing behind me?

Or am I just drunk?

I hiccup and snort and decide it's probably a mixture of both.

"How you holding up?" His breath skates across my collarbone and his tone, rumbly and sexy as hell, causes my abdomen to tighten.

I turn into him and his arm wraps around my middle, effortlessly, like two people in the middle of a dance where they both know the steps. Do we know the steps? Are we skipping all the awkward moments, the stepping on feet and not knowing where to place our hands? Is our connection that intuitive?

"I want you to take me home now," I whisper back, loving the way his eyes widen at the not-so-subtle message I deliver.

The green in his gaze darkens, less tropical rain forest and more mysterious wilderness. Even that sends a rush of heat through me, and I melt into his frame. His arms secure me fully and I press a kiss to the underside of his jaw, the tip of my tongue flicking out.

Scott laughs lightly, probably wondering why the hell I'm going all in on the PDA, but right now, I don't care about the repercussions. I'm an adult, an independent and capable woman who can certainly make my own choices about my love life.

"After you, sweetheart." Scott gestures toward the door.

I flash him a grin, catching my almost-stumble, as we turn to say our goodbyes. Scott leaves me in the warm embraces of the BHH girls while he grabs our coats.

"Thanks for coming out tonight." Indy hugs me.

"Thank you. And congrats," I say quietly.

She gives me another squeeze and then Abbi and Chloe are both hugging me from the sides.

"Get it, girl," Abbi jokes as Scott reappears, looking so effortlessly hot that I have to stifle my moan.

"No more tequila." I wag a finger at Panda.

"No promises," he quips back. He kisses my cheek and shakes Scott's hand. "Get home safely."

"Good game today," Scott tells him, and he grins.

After a few more waves and well-wishes, Scott bundles me into his car and drives us back to his place. During the drive, I shiver and he readjusts the heat, glancing at me.

"You okay?"

I nod, giving him a lazy smile. "More than okay. I had fun today."

"Me too." He says it like he's surprised by the admission.

I chuckle. "Don't you usually like watching the Hawks win?"

"Of course." He reaches over, his hand resting on my thigh. "But it was…different today. I had *fun*." He gives me another look. "And I'm glad the cupcakes were a success."

"Yeah," I agree. "That felt like a big win. I mean, I know I wouldn't have gotten the chance if—"

"Don't say that," he cuts me off. "You're a hard worker, Noelle. You have a great product and solid marketing and the personality to pull off introductions all on your own. Maybe it wouldn't have happened so quickly, but it would have happened. You can achieve whatever you set your head to."

His words both build me up and soothe an old wound and I sigh. "Thanks, Scotty."

"It's the truth."

"You're not just buttering me up for some hot sexy times?"

Scott barks out a laugh. His hold on my thigh tightens and I squirm.

"No. But I am trying to get home as quickly as possible for hot sexy times." He changes lanes and accelerates, giving me a quick wink. His hand slips higher up my thigh, slow and seductive and I wonder when he perfected this move.

I open my mouth to make a joke, but his fingers meet the apex of my thighs and every single one of my dumb, breathless, giggly thoughts fall straight out of my head. Scott's fingers work magic over the seam of my jeans, the friction, the visual, the damn road out the windshield, all more than I bargained for.

He changes lanes again and this time, it results in the button of my pants opening and the zipper dragging down. Then, he's cupping me and I'm shifting my hips forward to meet his touch. His fingers drag over my core like we have all the time in the world and for a moment, it seems like we truly do.

I glance at him only to be met with eyes that wreck me. Because for a blink, I see all the way to his soul. Sure, we're messing around. Yeah, it's fucking hot. But it's not a quick frenzy or a moment in time.

The look Scott gives me speaks to a forever that's so fulfilling, I gasp. His fingers slip under the silky material of my thong and glide through my arousal.

"Oh God," I murmur, suddenly sober. And wanting.

Between the looks Scott is flashing my way, the feel of his fingers playing over the most sensitive part of my body, the city rushing past outside my window, and the overwhelming sense that this is right, that this is perfect, pressure builds like a rolling wave. Higher and higher until I'm grinding against his hand, the seat belt cutting into my chest. Scott says my name like a plea, his attention solely on me as the car drives on autopilot. His gaze never leaves my eyes as he coaxes me higher, farther, to an insurmountable peak.

"Scott," I cry out, riding waves of bliss that continue to wrack my body as the car slows to a stop at a red light.

We're so close to the car next to us that if the driver glances our way, he would know exactly what we're up to. But neither of us cares. Neither of us looks away or moves. Scott's fingers still against my core. I continue to grasp the seat belt stretched between my breasts. Our panted breaths, mainly mine, fill the space.

I release a long exhale. "You're killing me, Scott."

"You're making me so goddamn happy, Noelle, I'm starting to think I've never been happy before."

His words slay me and, as he removes his hand from my underwear, I clutch it. His fingers are wet with my arousal, and it slips against my skin as I lace our fingers together. We ride like that the rest of the way to his house, with my open jeans, his confession, and a swirl of complicated, wanting, real feelings pulsing between us.

When we get back to Scott's, he wastes no time taking me, hard, fast, and fierce on his kitchen island. My ass grows numb as I sit on the edge of the counter, my fingers digging into Scott's flesh as I pull him closer, and he rocks into me.

Our bodies join like two puzzle pieces finally lining up, all perfect edges and a more complete picture. Our moans mingle, our hands continue the effortless dance of earlier, and I fall a little more for a man I should never want, never mind have.

"BAGEL OR TOAST?" I ask him the following morning.

He frowns, glancing at me over the copy of *The Atlantic* he's reading. "Good morning, beautiful."

I grin, mainly because I know that's a stretch. With my hair piled on my head, my eyes still half closed with sleep, and morning breath, I'm far from a morning beauty.

"I think we can do better than that," Scott says after a moment.

"What?"

"Pancakes or waffles?" he retorts.

"Oh," I laugh. "Waffles."

"I have a waffle iron."

"Have you ever used it?"

"What do you think?" He shifts, tossing down the magazine and turning onto his side to face me. His palm slides over the dip in my waist and rests there.

"Nope."

"Nope," he agrees, trailing kisses down the column of my neck.

I stretch my neck, giving him easier access, and roll onto my back. He follows, shadowing my body as my hands hold his sides.

"Pancakes?" I murmur, reminding him of our irrelevant conversation as he swings a leg over my body, straddling me.

"They're okay." His nose traces my jawline before he lines his mouth up with mine.

"Okay," I manage before he kisses me.

It's sweet, breathy, and the best way to wake up. As Scott slants his mouth over mine, I deepen our kiss, tugging him down until he's lying on top of me. We kiss, slowly, languidly, the way everyone should enjoy a Sunday morning. As our hands explore each other's bodies and our mouths savor each other's taste, I close my eyes and revel in the feeling. We make love, which is entirely different than the intense sex we had last night.

This is more appreciative, less frantic.

I press my head into the pillow as Scott grips the back of my thigh and hitches my leg higher. He sets a pace that slowly increases until we're both reaching for the stars and simultaneously shattering.

We come down slowly, a mass of limbs, uneven exhales, and beaming smiles.

"So, I'll make you waffles," Scott decides.

"I'd love that."

"I'd love it even more if you stayed."

I lift an eyebrow. "The day…?"

Scott studies me for a long moment, his thumb brushing over my cheek. "For much longer than the day, but we can start with that." He kisses me once before pulling himself from the warmth of bed.

I sit up slowly, wrapping the sheet around my chest and tucking it under my arms. He tugs on a pair of sweats but skips wearing a shirt. Truthfully, I'm glad, because the ways his muscles move should be appreciated by an ogler like me.

Scott catches me looking and grins. "I got a surprise for you."

"Really?" I ask, shifting forward. On my knees, the sheet twists around me like a strapless dress.

"It's not that exciting," he backtracks.

I lift my eyebrows, waiting.

He chuckles. "I figured out how to use the espresso machine."

Laughing, I fall back into bed. "Thank God for small miracles."

"See you in the kitchen, baby."

"See you there," I agree, watching his hot ass saunter out of the bedroom.

When I'm alone, I take a moment to savor the feeling. The bliss. The happiness of being completely and totally wrapped up in Scott's life.

Even the hockey parts.

CHAPTER 14
SCOTT

After a week of intense meetings, long conversations with Buck, and putting pieces in place to take a full twenty-four hours off, I'm in desperate need of a getaway with my girl. I spent Monday and Tuesday mostly in a daydream that Jayde delighted in calling me out on. Leaving her to handle any emergencies, I head to Primrose Sweets to scoop up Noelle for our much anticipated overnight.

"The majority of sales are cupcakes, but eclairs are sneaking up," Noelle says to the woman standing beside her.

I hang back, watching her in her element. Primrose Sweets has a line of customers, about eight deep, and I can tell business has picked up since the pop-up shop at The Meadows.

I grin and take a seat at one of the back tables. It takes about fifteen minutes, but as the last customers leave and the little bell over the door chimes, Noelle glances my way. Her face blossoms into a beautiful smile.

"You're here!"

I stand. "I am."

She tugs on the arm of the girl I assumed she's training, but now, I can see their familiarity with each other. The woman looks to be about the same age as Noelle but whereas

Noelle is all blonde ringlets and blue eyes, sunbeams and rainbows, this girl has black hair with pink streaks, an eyebrow ring, colorful arm sleeves, more edgy and wild. Kind of like Jayde.

"This is my best friend, Averie." Noelle presents the woman to me.

I give them a quick study, noting how in sync their movements are, even though they couldn't appear more different. It's a definite point for the old saying: opposites attract. These girls could be a billboard for it.

"It's the hair, isn't it?" Averie asks, quirking her brow with the barbell.

I shake my head. "No, it's more that I can see it." I gesture between them.

They both lift their eyebrows, waiting for me to continue.

I smirk. "Your connection. It's hard to miss." I hold out my hand to Averie. "It's good to meet you, Averie. I'm Scott. Thanks for coming to keep things here going so I can whisk this one away and try to impress her."

Averie grins and it's more like the sunbeams Noelle gives off. Yeah, they're definitely more like sisters. "You're off to a solid start."

Noelle scoffs and hip bumps her friend.

"Glad to hear it." I grin and tip my head toward the table. "Take your time; I'm ready whenever you are."

Noelle gives me an appreciative glance and rolls up onto her toes to kiss my cheek. "Thanks. I just need to check a few more things and then, I'm ready."

She scurries off for a moment and Averie gives me a look up and down.

"Ask away," I tell her, waiting for the inquisition. It's clear that she cares about Noelle, and if that means I have to answer some questions, I'll manage it.

"No." She shakes her head. "Just, be good to her. Everyone in Noelle's life is always trying to define it. From what she's told me, you just let her do her thing. Try to support it. You're good for her, Scott. I hope you guys enjoy New Orleans."

Surprise rolls through me at the honesty of her words, at how freely it was given. "Thanks, Averie. We'll bring you back some beignets."

She grins and again, I'm reminded of Jayde. Tough exterior but loyal to her core. "I'll hold you to that," she says as Noelle reappears with an overnight bag slung over her shoulder.

"No suitcase?" I wonder.

"Psh." She flicks a hand. "I travel light."

Averie snickers.

I hold out my hand and Noelle hands me her bag. As my arm practically drops to the ground, we all laugh.

"Light my ass," I joke as I walk toward the door. "Nice meeting you, Averie."

"See ya, Scott," she replies.

Noelle exchanges some last-minute reminders with her friend and then, I'm leading her toward my car, and we're heading to the airport.

"You ready?"

"I can't wait," she replies.

I reach over and as always, her hand finds mine. We ride to the airport in silence. I called ahead to make sure the jet would be fueled and waiting for our arrival. I want to maximize every second I can get with my girl.

As I pull into a parking spot, her phone beeps with a message.

She reads it and frowns, a little line appearing between her brows.

"Everything okay?" I ask.

She looks up quickly, as if I startled her. For a moment, her eyes are wide, frozen, like a deer caught in headlights. A tightness squeezes in the center of my chest. "What's—"

"Everything's fine," she rushes out, shaking her head. "All good." She tosses her phone back into her purse and tips her head toward the airport. "I'm ready for New Orleans."

"Hang on." I reach for her as she pushes the button to open the car doors. "You can tell me if—"

"It's my dad," she huffs out a breath. "And I don't want to ruin this overnight by talking about him."

I frown. "Why would it ruin anything?"

She shrugs, but when her eyes meet mine, they're pleading. "I just want to enjoy this time with you. Can't we stay wrapped up in us a little longer? Please?"

At the hopefulness in her expression, I acquiesce. "Of course, we can. But if you want to talk…"

"Not about Dad."

"Okay," I agree, giving her one more look. She seems okay, unaffected even. But something fusses in the back of my mind, a warning or a memory or something that doesn't want to be overlooked.

Still, when Noelle gets out of the car and grins at the waiting jet, I try to force the flare of unwariness away. Because I also want to remain wrapped up in us.

I grab our bags from the trunk and lead her toward the jet.

"Good morning, Mr. Reland," the flight attendant greets us as we enter the cabin.

"Morning, Sabrina. I'd like you to meet Noelle," I introduce her.

"Ms. DiSanto." Sabrina smiles pleasantly and guides us to our seats. "May I bring you something to drink before we take off?"

Noelle and I exchange a look, and at the glow in her cheeks, I shake off the wariness her father's message caused. "Champagne?"

She smiles and nods.

"Excellent." Sabrina walks away.

Noelle and I settle into our seats.

As I lean back into the plush leather and look at my girl, pulling a Kindle out of her purse, I love how normal it feels. Sure, the excitement of our first getaway is in the air, infusing the space with more excitement than a regular trip. But the vibe between Noelle and me is natural and easy, as if we've been doing this for years.

As if we've been a couple for more than a handful of weeks.

I know this is the first trip, I know things are new, but they feel like so much more than that. And suddenly, I want the whole world to know it, her father included.

Because I'm not messing around with Noelle DiSanto. I'm playing for keeps, and if her heart is the prize, then I want to earn it with zero uncertainties between us.

At some point, I know I'm going to have to go up against her father. For years, I've backed down when it comes to Rick DiSanto. Not so much in business, more in social settings. Noelle may be his daughter but she's my slice of happiness, and now that I've discovered it, I'm not willing to let her go.

Not without doing everything in my power to make things right. For me. For her. And most importantly, for us.

WE LAND in New Orleans in time for lunch, but I still want to start our trip with a traditional breakfast.

"What's better than a beignet and a coffee?" I ask my girlfriend who would never admit to drooling on my shoulder.

Noelle wipes the sleep from her eyes and manages a smile. "Definitely a coffee. If we only have twenty-four hours, I want to make the most of them."

"Me too, baby." I kiss the back of her hand, more than

ready to whisk her away for a day neither of us will forget and a night I hope we can repeat forever.

Christmastime in New Orleans is breathtaking. The city streets are decorated in red bows, lights adorn lampposts and balconies, and the city buzzes with its ever-present energy but at a heightened, hopeful level.

As we enter the French Quarter, I watch Noelle, enjoying the expressions that flit across her face.

"How many times have you been here?" I ask.

"A few," she responds, flashing me a smile. "I love the culture and of course, the food. It's almost like you can taste the soul—the resiliency of the people and the place—through the cuisine. It's all made with so much love."

"Exactly." I place my hand in hers as she voices my thoughts. She's got so much love and respect, so many big feelings for things I've either taken for granted or had no one to share them with, that I feel both lost and found when I'm with her. It's an unsettling feeling because I want to appreciate each moment we have together while also moving forward. And sometimes, it feels like I'm a lot more forthcoming with those wishes than Noelle is.

As we turn onto Bourbon Street, Noelle squeezes my hand and I let my thoughts settle. I don't want to interrupt this moment, or ruin today, with serious discussion. Instead, I want to enjoy New Orleans, see it through Noelle's eyes, and catch some of that Christmas magic I haven't felt in years.

As Noelle chats with my driver in fluent French, I turn to glance out the window. The colorful houses and balconies boasting with greenery pass by as her perfectly accented French and Ramon's slow, languid accent washes over me.

I relax more than I have in a long time, sinking back into the seat, lulled by the cadence of their conversation. Twinkling lights and red ribbons flash by outside, and even though I'm miles away from Boston, I feel at home.

I squeeze Noelle's fingers and without saying a word, I know it's her. I'm at home wherever she is.

CHAPTER 15

NOELLE

"I love this city," I tell Scott as we walk around Jackson Square. Even in the middle of the afternoon, in December, there're people milling about. It's better to be outside in a city like New Orleans, where the atmosphere has its own energy that seems to carry you like a wave.

The soul of the city is present in the delicious scents of Cajun and Creole cuisine wrapping around us. It's in the jazz that softly plays from open doors and cracked windows. It's in the resilient smiles of passersby and the warm invites to join, share, and celebrate.

"Me too. Even more so with you," Scott tells me as we pass through the gates and back onto the street. "You getting hungry?"

"Again?" I lift an eyebrow, recalling the beignets we inhaled an hour ago. But my stomach grumbles and Scott arches a questioning eyebrow back. "Yes."

He chuckles and takes my hand. "I've got a place I think you'll like."

We walk a handful of streets until we're back in the French Quarter, surrounded by everything I love most about this city: history, culture, and a hint of a French appreciation I could lose myself in.

When Scott walks me up to a small, light blue house on a corner, I nearly groan at the delicious scents wafting onto the street, beckoning us in like the enchanting magic and alluring voodoo shops dotting the area. The place is understated, with no sign, and the appearance of being half forgotten.

Which I soon realize couldn't be further from the truth. We walk inside and the jovial atmosphere of the restaurant, at capacity without an empty seat in the place, rushes to greet us. It's loud, boisterous, and enchanting.

I look up at Scott, his green eye sparking. "How'd you find this place?"

He grins, his lips twisting playfully. "Can't tell you all my secrets on our first getaway, Noelle."

"This is a gem," I continue.

"Best kept secret in town," he agrees, waving.

I turn to look over my shoulder and am met with the sincere, wide smile of a woman with an apron tied around her waist, and bracelets decorating her wrists. "Scott Reland! My God, it's been too long." She wraps Scott in a huge hug, the gold beads interspersed throughout her braids clinking together, like a champagne cheers on New Year's. "Come on, let me find you a seat. You needed some of my famous gumbo like yesterday."

"I missed ya, Angelique." Scott kisses her temple affectionately.

Angelique beams and turns toward me, her eyes narrowing as she sizes me up. The protective edge she seems to exert over Scott makes me like her even more and I smile reflexively, feeling my cheeks ache.

After a moment, Angelique laughs, the sound loud and uninhibited. She wraps an arm around my waist and turns us all toward a table that magically appeared in a back corner.

As she walks us toward the seats, patrons at other tables call out praise for their entrees or stop to clasp hands with Scott and exchange pleasantries.

"You're popular," I gush.

"Me or him?" Angelique tilts her head.

"Both of you," I admit.

She laughs again, the sound easy. "Scott's been coming here for years. In fact, this place never would have endured after Katrina if it wasn't for him but—"

"Angelique makes the best food in the French Quarter," he interjects, talking to me over her head, his cheeks suddenly tinged with color.

Angelique snorts and hugs him tighter for a second before releasing us both. "Think you can keep up?" she asks me.

I blush, wondering the full meaning behind her words.

"The drinks are strong," she warns, and I laugh.

"*Laissez les bon temps rouler*," I say heartily, loving the Cajun French expression about letting the good times roll.

Angelique chuckles, her dark eyes flashing. "You better hang onto her," she tells Scott. "I'll be back."

Then, she's swept up into the crowded restaurant, and Scott and I are seated at a small table, our coats discarded on the backs of our chairs, our cheeks aching from a day filled with laughter.

"I like it here," I say, looking around the space, taking in the photographs on the walls, celebrations of history and showcases of local artists.

"I'm glad." Scott looks at me for a long moment, the tone of his words conveying so much more than this restaurant.

Suddenly, it's as if we're talking about us, the future. My stomach tightens at the thought, but I don't want to consider it too closely right now. Not when Angelique brings us bowls of gumbo and large, red-colored cocktails, I know better than to ask for specifics about.

"Cheers." I pick up my glass.

"To you," Scott counters, clinking his against mine before taking a long pull.

I follow suit and nearly choke as the liquor coats my throat. Blinking back tears, I manage, "This is strong."

"You can handle it," Scott quips.

I roll my eyes and dig into the gumbo, moaning in appreciation. "This is amazing."

"I know," he agrees. "Wait 'til you try the crawfish. Oh, and the oysters. Angelique's cooking is renowned."

"How'd you find this place?" My curiosity gets the best of me.

Scott shakes his head, biting the corner of his mouth. "I didn't. I found Angelique. Years ago, when I was still playing baseball in college. Her mother's restaurant was in hard times and she was trying all these different recipes, whipping up ideas left and right, to try to draw a crowd. After a night of these"—he picks up his drink and shakes it at me before taking a sip—"I asked her if she'd ever want to run her own kitchen. She laughed and laughed, as if the idea was ludicrous. But after things took off with the Hawks, I came to see her and…the rest is history."

"History, huh?" I read between the lines, understanding that Scott put up at least some of the funds to support the restaurant.

"Everyone deserves a shot at their dreams, Noelle." His tone holds an undercurrent, as if he's speaking about me, the bakery. I narrow my eyes. "And everyone has help achieving them."

I nod slowly, realizing he's right. Even when you hustle and grind, there's always support propping you up. Whether it be financial or emotional or educational, it exists. "You're right."

"I know," he agrees cockily, and I laugh. "I'm glad I could

take you here. It's one of my traditions, to come every time I'm in town. But I always come this time of year."

"Because of the holidays?"

"Yes. Christmastime in New Orleans is sacred. It's an amazing celebration, but it's also humbling—a good reminder to count your blessings. To be grateful for the people you're breaking bread with and to enjoy the meal, the moment, the conversation. My life in Boston is usually rushed, hectic. But whenever I come here, I slow down and I remember, appreciate, how damn good it all is."

"I like that," I say softly. "I like that this is your place."

"Yeah." He takes a big bite of gumbo and groans, closing his eyes as he savors the tastes.

"What other traditions do you have?"

His eyes pop open, deep green and piercing. "For Christmas?"

"Or New Year's…"

Scott chuckles and shakes his head. "Not many. When I was a kid, my family gathered for Christmas Eve, and we went to Church at midnight. Then, presents in the morning."

"Yeah," I agree, recalling a similar childhood.

"But after Dad passed, Mom started visiting her sister for the holidays. My aunt and cousins live in Washington state. I'd usually try to make a trip out there but the last few years, with the Hawks schedule, it got too hectic." He winces as he says the word again, as if saying it out loud makes him realize how much he's missing out on. Scott shrugs. "I usually order in. No, don't give me that look." He wags a finger at me, and I school my expression, realizing too late that I was giving him a sad look. "But I always, always, have a carrot cake during the holidays. My grandmother used to bake one and she'd add her own secret ingredient. Cranberries." His eyes take on a faraway look, as if recalling an old memory. "But none have ever measured up to my grandma's." He shrugs. "Anyway, I told Mom I'd be staying put again this year. We have a game in Los Angeles on the twenty-third and...well, it's a choice I made."

"What if I asked you to make a different one?" I blurt out.

Scott lifts an eyebrow, waiting.

"Come home with me. For Christmas. I want you to celebrate with me and meet my dad as more than...well, as my boyfriend." The words are bold for me to make, but they feel right. I want them to be right, so I don't regret saying them.

Scott stares at me for a long moment, until I begin to fidget under the intensity of his gaze. "Yeah?"

"Yes."

"I'd love that, Noelle. The Christmas dinner, the time with you in New York, and being introduced as your man."

"Then, it's settled." I pick up my drink, as if cheers-ing to this makes it all real.

"Settled," Scott agrees, clinking our glasses once more.

We both drink slowly, our eyes holding over the rims of our cups.

"Stop making googly eyes at each other long enough to appreciate the heart and soul that went into these crawfish," Angelique announces, placing a big plate in between us with a thud.

I jump back in my seat, some of my drink dribbling down my chin. Scott laughs, his eyes wide as I snort, slapping a napkin over my chin. Soon, we're both hysterically laughing, unable to contain our sheer joy for this moment and the promise of a future that's sparking to life.

"SKIING OR SKATING?" I ask Scott as we walk down Royal Street. The walk is necessary after our heavy meal, and the cool breeze coupled with the twinkling lights makes the stroll romantic.

"Snowboarding," he responds.

"Really?" I turn to glance at him.

He nods. "You?"

"Skiing."

Scott smirks. "Christmas or New Year's?"

"New Year's. I like the idea of new beginnings."

"Same," he says. "Christmas kind of makes me sad, to be honest."

I tighten my hold on his hand and he smiles.

"But I'm looking forward to this year," he adds.

"So am I. Big parties or small—" I stop talking as I note the group of people swaying in the middle of the street. The sweet, melancholy notes of the trumpet hit my ears and I stop walking, letting the music and the visual of swaying bodies hold me captive.

"Come." Scott tugs my hand.

For a moment, I want to protest as I want to enjoy this for a bit longer. The music, the feelings it emits, the group of people lost to their own collective memories, but then I realize Scott is pulling me closer.

I go willingly as he brings me right into the group, his strong arms wrapping around me protectively as we begin to dance.

A group of kids swirl around us, their innocence and energy contagious. I smile and rest my cheek against Scott's shoulder. "I forgot you dance."

"What?" He fakes surprise, the laughter in his chest rumbling against my ear. "I guess I didn't do a good enough job making an impression over the summer," he murmurs the words quietly but in the next moment, he spins me out into the crowd with a move I didn't see coming.

I laugh and immediately, the music changes, an upbeat tempo that encourages clapping and cheers. As the other music revelers dance to match the beat of the music, the handful of children jump up and down around us.

I shake my head, my own laughter bubbling out of me, as Scott twirls me around in the heart of New Orleans. The inky sky watches over us, the Christmas lights flicker around us, and Scott's strong hands center me as I close my eyes, lift my face, and breathe in possibility.

CHAPTER 16
SCOTT

Being in New Orleans with Noelle is unlike any trip I've ever taken, whether alone, with friends, or with a woman. Mainly because I've never been with anyone like her, and seeing the city through her eyes, getting to experience my favorite places with someone I admire so much, fills the experience with added emotions.

As the song we're dancing to ends, I gather her against my chest and press my mouth against hers. It's a searing kiss, one that holds all the words I want to say but keep holding back. It's not unlike our first kiss, so many years ago, but there's an edge now. A want I can't douse because now that I've had her, I don't want to let her go. Noelle's not ready for the type of commitment, for the forever, that I want and I'm trying to tread lightly.

But hell if it isn't hard. Not when she looks like her, with angelic blonde curls and blazing, fierce eyes. Not when she's wrapped up in a sexy dress and western boots. Not when she's shown the same appreciation and admiration for the places that mean so much to me.

Her arms snake around my waist, pulling me closer. I tilt my head and her lips part, letting my tongue slip inside. Her mouth is warm and welcoming and even though I try to block it out, the word *home* blares through my mind like the trumpet now singing a sexy, slow tune.

Noelle's palm flattens in the center of my back and I feel the material of my shirt tug as her fingers curl into it.

I end our kiss softly before pulling away. "I need to get you home now," I tell her, desperately wanting to continue this, but not here, with all these onlookers and the delightful shrieks of school kids.

"Let's go," she agrees.

I kiss the tip of her nose once before releasing her. I dip into my wallet and add some bills to the tip jar of the band who set up shop on the curb, playing for the sheer enjoyment of the people who line the streets. "Thank you. That was beautiful," I tell them truthfully.

The guitar player whistles low, giving me a smirk. "So's your girl."

I laugh, turning to glance at my angel. "Yeah, she's special."

"Best get out of here now," he encourages, probably reading the longing in the lines of my face.

I nod and stride toward Noelle. Taking her hand, we walk the rest of the way to the cozy apartment I own in the city. Laying her down in the center of my king-sized bed, I open another part of my heart as I invite Noelle into more of my life, hoping with a reckless desire that she decides to stay.

Her skin is like silk when I run my hand down her calf, tugging off her boots. She props herself up on her elbows, giving me a lazy smirk, but she bites her bottom lip as I slide the skirt of her dress higher up her thighs.

When my hands cinch her waist, she giggles and flops back, her hair fanning out in an enticing spray of spirals. I hover over her, kissing her hard, and the sweetness of what we started on the street in the French Quarter turns steamy.

Noelle wraps her legs around my torso as I deepen our

connection, my hand splayed along the side of her neck, my mouth dragging, nipping, pressing kisses down the column of her neck. She arches into me, and I find her mouth, our lips fusing together as I kiss her deeply.

Her hands drop to my belt and as she sits up, I'm able to roll her dress up her frame until it clears her head and she's sitting before me, topless, all smooth skin with a spray of freckles.

"Brave," I comment, my forefinger hooking under her right breast, as if testing its weight. "Going bra-less."

She chuckles, the sounds musical. "I was hoping we'd end up here."

I grin, easing her back down as I pull off my sweater and discard it. "Were you having any doubts?" I lay beside her, hitching her leg up, my hold on the back of her thigh firm.

She shakes her head slowly, the tip of her nose grazing my jawline. And it's that movement, so simply and yet more intimate than what I'm used to sharing, that spurs me to act. To turn my head and kiss her hard, to help kick off my jeans when she works them down my legs, to grab her waist and help her settle over me as she works me up faster than any woman before.

With my arms pinned overhead and the thin lace of her panties moving up my abdomen, her breasts swing into my line of vision and I'm able to buck up enough to suck one pert nipple into my mouth.

Noelle moans, moving lower, allowing me to suckle, to swirl my tongue around the nub until it's glistening. She loosens her hold on my wrists and I press a palm into the center of her back, rolling her until we're side by side, a mass of limbs and desperate hands.

She rubs down my length, already rock hard and needy for her. My fingers dip into her, wet and so fucking sweet.

"Scott," she whispers, my name a breathless moan.

I drag her sweetness up around her clit and set a slow

pace, letting her know I want to do this all night. We're not in a rush. We have all the time, our whole future, all the tomorrows ahead of us.

She moves more forcefully against my hand, and I chuckle, moving my fingers to match her movements before I slide down her body and replace my fingers with my tongue.

"Oh God," she cries out.

My hands grip her thighs to hold her in place as I lap at her need, loving how fucking wet she is for me. My dick twitches against the material of my boxers but I ignore it, focusing on Noelle and her need.

Her moans grow in intensity, and I add two fingers, curling them inside of her and thrusting slowly, each movement in sync with the pace of my mouth. Within moments, Noelle shatters on my tongue and I look up, watching the sheer awe, the pleasure, the desire that ripples over her expression.

"You're so fucking beautiful," I manage to say.

Her eyes find mine and hold, too intense to blink away from.

"I'm falling in love with you, Scott," she tells me seriously, surprise laced in her voice.

I inch my way back up her body, pausing every now and then to kiss or nip an inch of her skin. She curls into me, her hands on my chest, slowly sinking lower.

"That's good, beautiful girl," I murmur when my lips meet her neck. I kiss the spot behind her ear, and she shivers. "Because I love you." I pull back to see her face, memorizing the awe that fills her eyes. "So fucking much, Noelle."

A smile crosses her mouth, slowly, delicately, and so damn sweet it steals my breath.

"I love you," she whispers as I kiss her hard.

Then, I slide inside of her and nearly die because her body is so fucking perfect; she's so fucking good. My mind short-circuits and pure need takes over. I set a pace that has her spilling sweet nothings and swears into my mouth, but I don't let up. Instead, I drive both of us higher until we peak and crash over the edge, free-falling into a future too bright to look at.

"THIS IS BETTER than I could have dreamed up," Noelle comments, wrapped in one of the handful of knit robes I keep in the closet. It's too big on her, the sleeves rolled several times, and still, she looks sexy.

I've called one of my favorite delivery places for takeout and we're sitting on the floor, around the living room coffee table, lounging in robes and slippers.

Too sexually sated to dress for dinner, I agreed when Noelle mentioned takeout. Even though I made dinner reservations, I'd rather be tucked away from the world with her, with no distractions but the ones we invent for ourselves.

"The sex or the food?" I joke.

She laughs, using her thumb and pointer finger to pick up a long piece of fettuccini and drops it into her mouth. "The food, obviously."

I snort and toss a piece of bread on her plate.

She grins devilishly and takes a long sip of wine. "This overnight, New Orleans, you, all of it."

"I know what you mean."

"Even Christmas. This time of the year, I forgot how magical it can be. How special it is when you have someone to truly celebrate it with."

I nod, feeling her words like a sucker punch. "The magic of the holidays."

"Exactly. When I was little, my mom used to gift me a

Waterford crystal ornament every Christmas. The box was always tucked into my stocking, and I would open it dutifully and mumble thank you but I never thought they were anything special. I used to wonder why she even bought them for me because they never went on the tree. And then, when she died, my dad explained it was so that one day, I could put them on my tree, and remember all the Christmases I spent with her." A sheen of tears coats her eyes and I sit up straighter, leaning forward so I don't miss a word. Not when she's being so vulnerable and real with me. "I have nine ornaments. They're beautiful. And I've never put them on a tree because it hasn't truly felt like Christmas since she passed. Not until now." She gives me a sad smile and my chest literally aches for her.

I shift around the table to pull her into my arms, wishing I could keep her there for always. "Let's get a Christmas tree, baby. Let's put them up."

She nods against my chest. "I'd like that, Scott."

"Me too." I kiss the top of her head, her curls tickling my nose. "That's a beautiful memory and tradition."

"Yeah."

"Let's start a tradition of our own, too."

Noelle pulls back to look up at me, her expression curious. "Like what?"

"Like…we buy an ornament on each of the trips we take together. Any place we go together, we get one to remember it by."

Noelle smiles, her eyes brightening as her emotion turns to excitement. "Okay. Let's do it. Tomorrow, we gotta find an ornament of a fleur de lis—"

"Or a beignet."

She laughs. "Definitely a beignet."

I kiss her. "Tomorrow morning. After brunch."

"Oof, more food?" She gestures to the Italian takeout opened across the coffee table.

I pinch her side. "It's only twenty-four hours, beautiful. Enjoy it."

She turns in my arms, her hands brushing against the back of my neck. "I am." Her voice is husky before she kisses me, initiating all the thoughts in my head.

I shift back so she can take control and have her way with me.

And it's a million times better than Italian takeout. Or a beignet.

CHAPTER 17
NOELLE

"I wish we found an ornament," I lament as we board the flight back to Boston the following morning.

"I can't believe we overslept," Scott says, his hand in the small of my back to guide me.

"I can," I admit, recalling all the deliciously naughty things we did last night. In Scott's bed. On the living room floor. In the shower. And then, the kitchen table.

My cheeks burn and I dip my head so Sabrina won't notice as she calls out a cheery greeting.

"Just coffee for me, please," I mutter as I drop into a seat, placing my purse on the seat across from mine.

"Same." Scott exchanges a few words with Sabrina.

I change my phone to airplane mode and settle back, watching Scott unfold his long body into the chair beside mine. He rolls the back of his head along the headrest, his eyes latching onto mine. "You have fun?"

"You know I did."

"You happy you're with me?"

"More than I thought I'd be," I joke.

He snickers and I smile. Our gazes hold, and for a breath, I lose myself in him. Is this what it's like? Being in love? Like floating and falling.

For years, I swore I wanted out of the hockey lifestyle but with Scott...could it be different? My dad never did fun overnights in cities across the country. He never made time to check out local artists or eat street food. Is Scott's version of owning a team different than what I know? Or does it just feel that way now, because this is new? Because this is...everything I've never had?

"For you, Noelle," Sabrina says, untucking my tray and placing down a coffee with milk and sugar, as well as a plate with two beignets and a carefully wrapped box.

I look up, surprised.

"From Scott," she explains, before turning away.

I turn to look at Scott.

"Open it," he demands.

"When did you have time to buy beignets?"

"When you were in the shower." He reaches down into his carry-on to pull out a bag with more beignets—"For Averie" —and a box of pralines—"and for you."

I tip my head back and laugh. This man. He's too damn much and he has no idea. How does he have no idea?

I pick up the box and unseal the seam of wrapping paper.

"Ah, come on now, dig into it properly. Like a kid who likes Christmas," Scott teases.

Grinning, I do as he says and rip off the paper, a thrill shooting down my spine. When I open the box, I gasp. Nestled inside is the most beautiful Christmas ornament of a...wait for it, beignet... the powdered sugar a delicate sprinkling of shimmering glitter that catches the light. I laugh but tears spring to the corners of my eyes because—"This is beautiful." I turn to the man beside me. "And so damn thoughtful."

He cups my cheek, his thumb swiping up my cheekbone. "I love you, Noelle."

The words are more than a declaration, they're a promise. So sincerely given that they fill me with lightness, with hope.

Scott presses his mouth to mine in a simple kiss. "Check the ribbon," he whispers.

I turn my attention back to the ornament and run my fingers along the ribbon on the ornament. My eyes nearly fall out of my face when I catch sight of the two diamond earrings pinned into place on either side of the shimmering beignet. "Scott," my tone is hushed, half in awe, half in shock. "What did—"

"Do you like them?"

I look up at him, taking in his expectant expression. "Are you kidding me? These are...they're breathtaking. They're beautiful. They're way too much and—"

"Put them on. Let me see you in them."

My fingers tremble as I do what he says. "I can't believe you...these must be a carat each," I blurt out.

He chuckles and helps take out one of the earrings. "One and a half."

I give him a look and his laughter grows.

I put the earrings on and turn my head, tilting my neck to flash him the diamonds. When I glance at him, I expect to see his mirth, but instead, his eyes are bold and serious. Smoldering.

He reaches up slowly and runs the pad of his thumb over one diamond. "I want to cover you in these," he murmurs, his tone low.

A shiver works down my body at his words, at the meaning behind them.

"Scott—"

"I mean it, Noelle. I want this with you."

"We'll be taking off now," the pilot announces as Sabrina reappears and runs through the pre-flight instructions and safety precautions.

I settle back in my seat and lace my fingers with Scott's, his words ringing in my head.

I want to cover you in these.

I want this with you.

Diamonds. They signify marriage, commitment, forever.

I peek up at Scott, studying the clench of his jaw, the twitch of his lips, the various expressions that cross his face as he reads an article in *The Atlantic*.

Can we create a forever? Or will hockey eventually come first?

I RECEIVE my answer in the following weeks. At first, the glow of our trip clings to everything, brightening my entire world. The future holds promise and excitement. I wonder why I was so hesitant about getting involved with Scott in the first place. After all, when things are this good, I'd be a fool to question it. Even Averie, more skeptical in nature than me, gushed over the diamond earrings and swooned over the beignets he remembered to bring her.

But after Averie went back to New York, my real life took over. Boston, the bakery, the intensity of my schedule expanded and dimmed the radiance I was caught up in. After the second time Scott cancelled plans with me, I started questioning everything. Doubt began to color the memories of our time in New Orleans. Was that just a moment in time? Is real life with Scott the type of lifestyle I want to avoid?

With only two weeks until Christmas, time seems to simultaneously speed up and slow down. My days at the bakery are long, with cold early mornings cloaked in darkness, and late nights wrapped in sugar and cinnamon and memories.

While the time I spend with Scott grounds me in a way I've never experienced before, our midnight meet-ups showcase just how out of sync our schedules are.

Two days ago, I had to cancel our lunch plans and when we finally caught up last night, emails about opening new pop-up shops in other arenas dictated my night. I think Scott wanted to talk about something regarding the Hawks, and while a tinge of guilt flared in my chest that I didn't have time to listen, I also felt too overwhelmed to worry much about it.

I flip the lock on the bakery door and pull my phone from my back pocket. Frowning, I realize I missed a call from Scott forty minutes ago. I click on the text message he sent, my heart sinking when I realize we aren't having dinner tonight. We were supposed to. He swore it after I had to cancel lunch.

But we were also supposed to put up a Christmas tree and decorate it with my mother's ornaments which still hasn't happened. In fact, we haven't spoken of it again since New Orleans.

SCOTT

Beautiful girl, one of my players needed
some advice. I'm boarding a flight to
Tennessee. Be back early in the morning.
Sleep at my place tonight. I miss you.

Leaning against the door, I tilt my head back and close my eyes. New Orleans and beignets and diamond earrings were only two weeks ago, and in some ways, it feels like a lifetime. Because since we returned from our trip, we both hit the ground running.

Orders at the bakery have quadrupled. In addition to our daily stock, I've been baking for birthday parties, office holiday gatherings, as well as home games at The Meadows. Scott's in the midst of the season, traveling to away games every week, as well as providing support to his players—like this last minute trip to Tennessee—that Dad never offered.

While a swell of pride rises inside of me over the type of owner, the kind of man, he is, I can't help but feel like I'm back to playing second fiddle. The same way I did for most of my childhood, ever since Mom passed.

Sighing, I drag my eyes open and force myself to go through the motions of closing out the register, doing the final cleanup and prep for tomorrow morning, and saying good night to Primrose Sweets.

I'm pulling my hair out of the back of my winter coat when my phone rings. I fumble with it, my hope skyrocketing and crashing when I realize it's not Scott, but Dad, on the line.

"Hi, Daddy," I answer.

"Noel, noel…" he sings the opening lines of "The First Noel."

Despite my mood, I smile. "How are you?"

"Good, now that I know you'll be home in a week."

"Ha! I see what you did there. But yes, I'll be home in ten days, Dad. I—"

"Come earlier. I've barely seen you these past few months and you know how hectic things are before the holidays. I've got some meetings lined up that I'd like you to be part of," Dad rattles on, giving more details about the meetings but I'm already tuning him out.

Isn't he happy Primrose is doing so well? Doesn't he understand that I don't want to continue his legacy with the Sharks?

"…give him a chance, honey. He's a great guy and—" Dad's still talking but his mention of Ben Tully gets my attention. I thought he would have gotten the hint when I blew off his text message.

"I'm seeing someone," I cut him off.

"Noelle—" Dad's voice grows serious, and I know that whatever he's about to say is something I don't want to hear.

"It's Scott. And it's serious." I shut him down.

A few moments of tense silence follows, and my heart rate

ticks up. Even though I'm an adult, even though my dad has no say in my dating life, I still want his approval. I still want him to be proud of me. Happy for me. I clench my phone tighter, waiting for him to respond.

He clears his throat. "Scott Reland."

"I've invited him home for Christmas," I whisper, wondering if I'm rushing things. In a handful of weeks, I told Scott I love him and asked him to come home with me for the holidays. Those are big steps and…things are changing, shifting, so quickly. Did we move too fast? Is the novelty of us already wearing off?

New Orleans and beignets and diamonds flash through my mind.

But when we were there, everything felt right. It *felt* natural and organic and true.

Then why am I questioning it now? Because of two weeks of being busy?

"Is he why you can't come home earlier?" Dad growls and I focus back on the conversation and the anger in his tone. "Is Scott already dictating your time with your family? Putting the Hawks over the Sharks?"

I shake my head, trying to clear it from…what? The absurdity of this conversation? "Dad, no, I'm working. I want to keep the bakery open until the twenty-second."

Dad scoffs. "Scott can't come on the twenty-second. The Hawks are in Los Angeles on the twenty-third."

As soon as he utters the words, my heart sinks and I pull out a nearby chair to plop down on it. Ignoring Dad, I pull the Hawks schedule up on my phone and realize he's right, remember that Scott said as much in New Orleans.

Are we even going to put up a Christmas tree? A lump forms in my throat and I swallow against it.

I'm overthinking this. I am totally overreacting. It's just that…Scott and I spent a magical night in New Orleans and since then, real life has smacked us in the face, a daily reminder of all the obstacles we're up against.

In some ways, Dad is the least of the hurdles I need to jump.

"Well, I'll be there on the twenty-third," I say, an edge to my voice that I know Dad hears because he clucks his tongue.

"Good. Then you can have dinner with me at Franklin's Steakhouse that night. We can spend some time together, me and you. I need to remind you that you're still a Shark, no matter who you're dating in Boston."

I roll my eyes but acquiesce. Dad and I haven't spent time just the two of us in ages, and as I turn the idea over in my mind, I realize I'd like to see him without Scott too. "I'll meet you at Franklin's."

"I'll make the reservation for 8 p.m."

"Okay."

"Let me hear a smile," Dad demands.

Reluctantly, I chuckle.

"There she is. Miss you, my Noelle."

At the affection in Dad's tone, I soften. "Me too, Daddy. I'm looking forward to dinner. And Christmas. So, please, for me, give Scott a chance."

Dad clears his throat and mutters something I don't catch but wishfully think is a reluctant agreement.

"See you soon," I tell him.

"Good night, honey."

After hanging up with Dad, I check my messages again, even though Scott is still flying. Shaking off my disappointment, I pocket my phone and make my way home.

Even though he said I should sleep at his place, tonight, I want my own bed. My own space. My own thoughts and emotions, so I can sift through them without his scent and the shadow of his presence hovering over me.

I miss Scott Reland, but I also know this is just the beginning. This is the life of a hockey wife.

CHAPTER 18
SCOTT

"Congratulations, Scotch." I shake hands with Noah.

"Never would have got this deal off the ground without you, Scott." He clasps my shoulder with his other hand, his eyes serious.

"You would've," I tell him truthfully. "Maybe not this quickly," I half joke and he grins, tapping my shoulder with a closed fist. "But you would've. I'm proud of you, man."

"Thank you," he says, before embracing his father-in-law and Torsten in congratulations.

Together, the three men, along with Torsten's brother and cousins in Norway, just signed on the dotted line. They bought the Tennessee Thunderbolts and will begin next season as NHL team owners and hockey coaches instead of former players.

"Thanks for your help on this, Scotty." Jeremiah shakes my hand.

"Anytime," I tell my childhood idol. "I'm happy for you guys."

"Me too. I wanted this," he admits, looking around the arena. "One more shot to leave my mark…to leave my grand-kids something special." He gestures toward the ice.

Scotch shakes his head good-naturedly while Torsten winks. I tip my head toward the ice and tell Jemmy, "This is more than special."

My phone buzzes and I slip it from my pocket, hoping it's Noelle. My hope dies when I read Jayde's name on the screen. Gesturing to the men that I need to take the call, I step into the hallway.

"What's up, Jayde?"

"Tennessee?" she asks.

I frown. "Yes. I'll be back tomorrow."

"Oh good. But your dinner reservations at La Maison were for *tonight*."

I scratch my forehead, trying to piece together what she's not saying. Who the hell cares if I missed cancelling a reservation? That's her job anyway. Except—"Shit."

"You never cancelled with Noelle," she correctly surmises.

"Damn," I mutter, feeling awful. I sent her a text to tell her I was coming down to Tennessee, but I completely forgot that we had dinner plans tonight. Dinner plans I swore we'd keep after she cancelled our last lunch and I missed dinner over the weekend. Instead of remembering, I asked her to crash at my place. I'm an asshole. I blow out a deep breath. "I—"

"Flowers or chocolates?" Jayde asks wryly.

I snort. "Neither."

"Correct. Jewelry is much better."

At Jayde's words, I recall the diamond earrings I bought Noelle in New Orleans. Was that only two weeks ago? It seems so much longer, especially since we've both been busy, caught up in our work schedules and commitments, from the moment the plane landed back in Massachusetts.

"I'll make it up to her," I say.

"I imagine so. I'm also calling about the game against Los Angeles on the twenty-third. Are you flying straight from California to New York for Christmas, or do you need to stop back in Boston first?"

I wince, realizing that Noelle and I haven't hammered out Christmas plans yet.

"And do you want to fly out the night of the twenty-fifth or morning of the twenty-sixth?" In the background, I hear the soft clacking of Jayde's fingers on the laptop keyboard. It sounds like a ticking sound, reminding me that I need to make decisions.

For years, I could rattle responses off the top of my head but now… "I'm not sure. Let me talk to Noelle."

"The twenty-fifth is better. You have a dinner with the Huxley brothers on the evening of the twenty-sixth."

I swear, scrubbing my palm over my hair. I forgot about that too. The Huxley brothers own part of an arena in Tennessee. Given the new owners of the Thunderbolts, I thought the arena could benefit from a pop-up stand of Primrose Sweets. But I didn't discuss it with Noelle yet.

"I'll get back to you," I tell Jayde, irrationally frustrated with her for being efficient while I'm mentally trying to recall my schedule.

"Okay," she says easily, sensing my annoyance. "See you tomorrow, Boss."

The line goes dead and I sigh, pinching the bridge of my nose.

"Hey, you up for a burger and a beer? There's a place I want to try." Torsten comes up behind me. His ice blue eyes glimmer with excitement at trying a new restaurant. A foodie at heart, he used to drag the team to every new restaurant opening in Boston.

More than anything, I want to get on a plane, go home to my girl, and climb into bed beside her. But at the happiness in Torsten's expression, not to mention the fact that he flew in from Oslo, I also want to take the rare opportunity to hang with these guys. To celebrate with them. They're now a part of the NHL owners circle and it feels good to be in the club together.

I just wish Noelle was here too.

But she's made it clear that she's not into the whole hockey thing. And I get that; hell, I even respect it. But she'll understand right? About the cancelled dinner? The last-minute flight? The missed calls and unanswered texts?

After all, I've never asked her to choose me, or us, over anything regarding her career. I've been nothing but understanding when things come up for her at the last minute. I know she doesn't want to be part of this world, but I'd still like her understanding and consideration for my career.

"Sure. I'd love that," I tell Torsten, grinning as he whoops and calls out to Scotch.

TO SAY I'm disappointed to see my perfectly made bed sans Noelle the following morning is an understatement. Was she just tired last night? Or is she pissed about the dinner reservation?

Either way, she's not here and I need a shower. And coffee.

I take a hot shower, dress, message Jayde that I'll be late this morning, and head to Primrose Sweets.

It takes me longer than usual to find parking and after swearing at a group of hungover college kids for making damn snow angels in the middle of the street, I finally park and make my way over.

Holy shit. I stop on the sidewalk, staring up at the sign. The line is out the door. Good for Noelle!

Pride fills me that her bakery has taken off so much, that her hard work is being recognized and appreciated. But as I stand on the sidewalk, with flurries swirling down from the gray sky, and freeze my balls off, I debate texting her to see if she can pop out and bring me a coffee.

No, I can't do that. She's busy, probably overwhelmed.

I wait for ten minutes, eavesdropping on the conversations unfolding around me before Jayde calls.

"I've got a latte on your desk and you're about to be late for your first appointment."

"Shit." I step out of the line and make my way back to my car. Before I slide behind the wheel, I glance at the bakery and wish I could catch a glimpse of Noelle. I miss her.

Of course I know I'm busy with work, but I've never dated a woman who had so much going on in her own life too. It makes it hard to hang out and see each other but downright impossible to do the last-minute, surprise hellos, that I've always enjoyed.

Another time, I tell myself. Then, I turn on my car and drive to work, vowing to make the last few days up to Noelle. As soon as I can fit it in.

"CHRIST, I MISSED YOU," I tell her that evening. The second my arms wrap around her, relief fills me up.

"Me too," she murmurs, giving me a peck. But then she steps out of my embrace and circles around me to the kitchen. "What do you feel like eating for dinner?"

"Takeout?" I turn, wishing she let me hold her for more than a heartbeat.

"Sure."

I pull out my phone. "What are you in the mood for?"

"Whatever." She shrugs.

I give her a look but at the casual expression on her face, I punch in an order for sushi. When I'm done, I toss my phone on the couch and follow Noelle into the kitchen. I really want to tell her about Tennessee, to confide in her about Scotch and the Bolts. To have her express interest in my workday, the way I always do with hers. "Noelle, I'm really sorry about the dinner reservations. Tennessee happened so last minute and you're never going to believe—"

Her phone rings and her eyes widen as she glances at it.

"Take it," I say automatically.

She gives me a pleading look. "I'm so sorry. I need to—"

"Of course." I gesture toward her phone, and she swipes it up.

"Averie? Yeah, what's wrong? Shit." Noelle begins to walk in front of the kitchen island, and I slip onto a barstool, listening to her side of the conversation in an attempt to piece the conversation together.

"He can't come tomorrow?" She stops walking. I sit up straighter. "Yeah, okay. How much?" She resumes walking. "Shit, yeah, I mean, it is what it is. Yep, I'll give him a call in the morning. Thanks, Aves. 'Bye."

"What happened?" I ask the second she ends the call.

She places her phone down and shakes her head. "The refrigerator and freezer stopped working at Primrose New York. We just got our inventory in and now, it's all wasted. The repairman can't come until the end of the week." She rubs the center of her forehead, as if trying to diffuse an oncoming headache.

"Shit, babe. I'm sorry to hear that." I pull out my phone, scrolling through my contacts. "Let me see who I know…"

"It's okay." She places her hand on mine. "It's not your problem."

I frown. Doesn't she realize we're in this together? I'm about to remind her when her phone rings again.

She rolls her eyes when she reads the screen. "Hi, Daddy."

I retake my seat on the barstool as she bickers with her father. They start talking about the bakery, but it quickly shifts into something else, with the name Ben Tully being said more than once. My jaw tightens and I feel the muscle under my left eye tick.

Watching her twirl a thick curl around her finger, I think about how much has happened since we returned from New Orleans. The deal in Tennessee. Noah Scotch's upcoming retirement that the world still doesn't know about. Noelle's massive growth at the bakery. The chance for her to expand into other arenas. And yet, Noelle and I haven't talked about any of it. We haven't shared our wins or discussed our worries. In fact, she barely asks about the things happening in my world, about anything connected with the Hawks.

We've been more like roommates than a couple for the past two weeks and while I recognize it's because we're both busy, I also know our schedules aren't going to magically free up anytime soon.

Which is why it's important we spend Christmas together. I need to be with her in New York for as long as I can.

A knock at the door signals that the sushi has arrived. I flash Noelle a smile as I go to answer the door. Once I lay out the sushi, I send Jayde a quick text.

SCOTT

Book the ticket from CA to NY direct. Return for the 26th. I want to stay in New York as long as possible.

JAYDE

Good call, Boss.

Of course Jayde can't help herself from weighing in on my relationship. I place my phone back down and wait for Noelle to finish her call so we can eat dinner. And, hopefully, talk about all the things we need to catch up on.

CHAPTER 19
NOELLE

By the time I hang up with Dad, Scott's on a call and our sushi is mostly forgotten. Shit.

I sit down and pick up a California roll. Using my fingers, I dunk it into a small bowl of soy sauce and pop it into my mouth.

It sucks that the refrigerator and freezer went out at Primrose New York. It sucks even more that the inventory is wasted. While I have room in the budget to replace the inventory and repair the appliances, the issue is going to be timing. We're crazy busy during the holiday season and I don't want to lose the confidence of my customers by not delivering. I sigh, my irritation flaring. At this point, it's like I'm pushing them into the bakeries of my competitors.

"Hey," Scott's voice pulls me from my thoughts, and I glance up at him, pasting a smile on my face.

"Hi. Come eat."

He sits on the barstool next to mine, a long sigh leaving his body, as if he can finally relax for the first time today.

"Long day?" I ask.

He nods. "You?"

"The longest."

"I came by Primrose this morning," he says while adding edamame to his plate.

I turn to look at him. "You did?"

"Line was out the door." He bumps his arm against mine. "Proud of you, beautiful. You're doing an amazing job."

"Thanks, Scotty. Why didn't you come in?"

"I was waiting and—"

"You didn't have to wait."

He shrugs. "Didn't want to piss off your customers."

I laugh and pucker up to kiss his cheek. "My boyfriend takes precedence."

His expression grows solemn, and he takes my hand. "I'm glad to hear you call me that."

At the seriousness in his tone, my smile slips. "What do you mean?"

"These past two weeks have been…a lot."

Now, I sigh. "I know. And, to be honest with you, I don't know when it won't be a lot."

"Exactly," Scott mumbles. "Me neither. But we'll figure it out, right?"

I nod slowly. "I hope so."

"Hey, come on now." He bumps against me again. "We got this."

"I guess. I just…my only other relationship was with Chris. And both of our lives were so intertwined with hockey. Now, our lives are…"

"Separate."

"Yeah. But I like it that way."

He looks at me for a long moment, something I can't read rippling over his face. "Yeah," he says, neither a confirmation nor a denial. "Well, let's get through the holidays and we'll see what the new year brings."

"Right." I wince at the "getting through the holidays." Because you're not supposed to "get through" them, you're supposed to enjoy and savor them. Still, I know exactly what he means so I don't expand. Instead, we eat our sushi quietly and when his phone rings again, I'm almost relieved he needs to take the call.

As I watch him walk around the living room, his EarPods in his ears, his hands gesturing as he speaks, I can't help but wonder what the new year holds. For me, for him, for us.

Because right now, neither of us is giving the commitment necessary to be in a relationship. And yet…I don't want to be in a relationship with any man but him. Maybe I shouldn't be in a relationship at all.

AFTER ANOTHER WEEK of early morning goodbye kisses and late-night hellos with Scott, I post a sign that Primrose Bakery will be closed from the twenty-second through the Christmas holiday. It's one-hundred percent not a great business decision but I'm not willing to miss Christmas in New York with Dad.

Besides, Primrose New York will be swamped, and I'm trying to keep up with the inventory needs. I should be working there for the next few days. When I close the bakery, I lock the door for the last time this year. Then, I tug on my suitcase to wait for my Uber.

When I turn, I'm surprised to see my guy leaning up against his Tesla.

"Hey!" I call out, grinning.

"Hey yourself. Need a ride?"

"To the airport?" I guess.

"I want to see you off. I'm sorry I can't come with you but—"

"You'll be there after Los Angeles."

"Right after. I'm taking a direct flight." He grips the back of his neck. "If two of my players didn't end up in jail the last time we played in LA, I wouldn't even go. But this game could go sideways, so I need to be there."

"I get it. We'll celebrate in the city soon enough."

"Absolutely." He dips his head and kisses me hard. He stashes my suitcase in the trunk while I cancel my Uber.

Then, we head toward Logan International Airport and I stare out the window, reflecting on how much has changed since I came to Boston only a few months earlier. I successfully launched Primrose Sweets Boston and fell in love with Scott.

Rolling my head along the headrest, I look at him.

One side of his mouth tugs upward under my scrutiny. "Yes, beautiful girl?"

"Thanks for driving me."

"Of course."

"Take it easy on my dad over Christmas, okay? I want to enjoy this holiday with both of you and…"

"I got you." He squeezes my hand in acquiescence, but his jaw tightens. Still, I'll take it.

"Thank you."

He gives me a real smile and nods. We make small talk until we arrive at the terminal. There's not enough time to talk about any of the real things that have been happening over the past two weeks and neither of us wants to get into a serious discussion about our work or lives to have to cut it short.

When I step out of the car, I breathe in the cold winter air and turn to kiss Scott goodbye. He settles my suitcase next to me and gives me his signature smirk.

"See you in New York," he murmurs, brushing my curls away from my face.

"I can't wait."

"Me too, baby. Love you." He leans down and kisses me, slow and steady, reminding me that we got this.

"Love you too," I whisper when we pull apart.

"See you in a few days, Noelle."

"See you soon," I agree. Then, I wave one final goodbye, grip my suitcase, and enter the airport.

Two hours later, I'm on a plane headed for New York even though my heart is in Boston, with Scott.

"OKAY, GIRL, WHAT GIVES?" Averie asks me point-blank at happy hour. We're at one of our favorite spots, a local hangout on the Lower East Side that boasts standard chips and salsa, but renowned margaritas.

"What do you mean?" I deflect, dunking a chip and stuffing it into my mouth.

She rolls her eyes, undeterred. "Hot Hawks owner with a devilish smirk and a sense of style?"

I grin. Scott does have both of those things. "He's coming for Christmas."

"I know. What I don't know is why you aren't gushing about it."

"I'm happy he's coming."

She lifts a no bullshit eyebrow.

"I am," I swear. "Things have just been…off between us."

"Off how?" She bites noisily into a chip.

"We've both been really busy with work, and it feels like we're just not…connecting."

"But when you are together…?"

"Things are fine. Good. It's just we're never together for long enough to really talk about things. He has no idea that I've been invited to open pop-up shops at an arena in Houston and Los Angeles. I still don't know why he went to Tennessee and what player needed help. Or for what. Our days are overflowing with a million things to do that by the time we see each other at night, we're both too exhausted to do much but make small talk and have sex."

Averie laughs. "The sex part sounds pretty great."

"It is," I confirm.

"At least you got that going for you." She raises her margarita in my direction before taking a long gulp. "So, you're in a stable relationship with an incredible man who looks like the definition of sex and you're worried because you guys are both killing it at your careers?"

"Pretty much," I quip, realizing how lame I sound when Averie words it the way she just did.

She smirks. "Don't feel bad for having a good thing going, Noelle. I get what you're saying. You're worried that you guys aren't connecting the way you should be and if you can't connect now, when you're in the honeymoon phase, when will you?"

"Exactly."

"And New Orleans was all magic and hot sex and good food and his undivided attention but Boston is—"

"Reality." I sulk.

"Reality. But that's not a bad thing. I think you guys just need to carve out more time for each other and communicate. He probably has no idea you're feeling this way because he's just as busy as you are."

"That's the thing though; I know he's not going to get less busy. I've watched my dad for years, owning an NHL team is a lifestyle. One I never wanted any part of. And I'm not going to get less busy. Not when I'm trying so damn hard to expand and grow Primrose."

"True," Averie agrees.

"I just wonder if we have a real chance at this. It's already hard and…he and Dad haven't even buried their crap yet."

"Which is a goal for Christmas dinner," Averie points out, winking at me. "Great timing."

I scoff.

"Seriously," she says, "I think you're overthinking this. You've never been in a big-girl relationship before."

"I dated Chris," I remind her.

"Yeah, and it was easy because he played for your father, and you were always around. You didn't have to work to make it work."

"And he still cheated on me," I remind her again.

"He was a douche."

"I know."

"Scott's not."

"I know."

"You gotta talk to him, babe. Like an adult. A woman who has priorities and goals and isn't trying to sacrifice them but also wants to make it work with him. I don't think he's expecting you to give up on anything, not the way Chris and your dad—"

I give her a sharp look and she stops talking. Instead, she takes a huge gulp of her margarita and I follow suit.

"Just, talk to him," she repeats.

"I will," I agree, recognizing the merit in her advice. Scott's never tried to make me slow down or choose hockey over my bakery. If anything, he's been the most supportive person in my life save for Averie. "I want us to have an amazing Christmas together."

"You will," my bestie assures me. "You just need to be honest with each other. You need to talk. And over the holi-day, you should have uninterrupted time to do that."

"You're right," I agree.

She clinks her glass against mine. "I know. Now drink up. I'm already two drinks ahead of you."

I laugh and take a big pull of my margarita, suddenly feeling better than I have in over a week. Tomorrow, Scott will be in New York. At 2 p.m., Primrose New York will close for the Christmas holiday, and I'll be able to sit down and properly spend time with my man. We'll celebrate Christmas and start some of those new traditions we talked about. Together.

WHEN I ENTER FRANKLIN'S, my favorite steakhouse in Manhattan, the familiar atmosphere and soft background noise of patrons enjoying their entrees welcomes me. After a fun happy hour with Averie, I'm famished and ready to tuck into a big steak.

"There she is," the host, Miguel, greets me. He opens his arms and I step into them, grateful for the warm hug.

Given the bustle of the past few days, I'm looking forward to spending time with Dad. Being back here, in a place that is woven into many childhood memories and seems like a thread in mine and Dad's relationship feels right. Kicking it off with a hug from Miguel solidifies that.

"It's good to see you, Migs." I kiss his cheek before pulling back.

"Your Papa misses you," he remarks, his dimple flashing. Even though Miguel is likely around Dad's age, he hasn't aged the way Dad has. Miguel is still as fit and charming as the day I met him, when I was six. "It's good to have you home."

"Happy to be here." I glance toward the back of the restaurant, where Dad and I always sit. When I see our usual table is empty, I frown. "He's not here yet?"

"He is." Miguel fiddles with a stack of menus. "But you're at a four-top tonight. He's brought a guest, Ben Tully?"

My stomach sinks and, noting my obvious disappointment, Miguel makes a sympathetic cluck.

"Come on." His palm gently nudges me forward. "It

won't be that bad. I can ask Chef to mess with his dinner and—"

I chuckle and the tightness around Miguel's eyes eases as he smiles back. But then, his look grows serious.

"How do you like Boston?"

"I like it. I'm happy there." The words are honest and surprising because in the few months I've lived there, I've come to view Boston as home.

"Then be happy, *mija*," Miguel whispers, an edge to his tone. "Stay there."

I dip my head in acknowledgement, knowing that his uttering the opposite of Dad's wishes, especially when they're so well-known, is a risk. But Miguel has always had my back.

"Thanks, Migs."

He squeezes my shoulder, but as we step into the main dining area, his hand falls away. We both straighten our postures, don an air of professionalism, and walk toward the table where Dad and Ben await.

Dad beams when he sees me. He and Ben stand as I approach, and Ben slickly pulls out my chair.

"There she is," Dad announces, echoing Miguel's words but in a very different tone, "the future of the Sharks!"

Ben grins. "I look forward to the day."

Nausea balloons in my stomach. Miguel clears his throat. Ben leans forward and kisses my cheek, the scent of his cologne overpowering and nauseating.

I open my mouth to announce I have a boyfriend, Scott, but I don't want to seem childish so instead, I sit. And my mind spins as I try to make sense of Dad's blatant attempts to set me up with Ben and Ben's lame laughter at everything Dad says.

Miguel is right; I should stay in Boston.

I sit quietly for most of the meal, dutifully responding to questions when asked but not engaging in the conversation. I'm too preoccupied trying to process my hurt. Doesn't Dad want to spend time with me? Shouldn't my well-being and happiness come before his desire to marry me off to Ben?

Listen to your father, Noelle. I squeeze my eyes shut to dispel my mother's voice.

We're tucking into our steaks when Dad mutters something that catches my attention.

"Yeah, Scott Reland was part of that deal. New owner of the Tennessee Thunderbolts."

Ben scoffs. "A dying team. It was short-sighted of Reland to pour so much money into it."

"Not to mention the hours," Dad agrees. "He's going to put in some serious time down in Knoxville to turn things around."

"I wonder if he'll move there?" Ben asks, spearing a piece of steak.

My head spins, my throat dries, and I sit frozen in my seat, trying to play catch up.

Scott bought another hockey team? One he didn't tell me about? He might be moving to Tennessee?

Suddenly, everything flips upside down. My skin burns hot and cold and nausea rolls in my stomach. My chest aches and my stomach twists painfully, ending my appetite.

Was I fool to trust that things between Scott and me would be different? Or is this the moment I was waiting for, the one I knew would eventually come, the one that places hockey over everything?

CHAPTER 20

SCOTT

"What's wrong?" The words tumble out of my mouth the moment I spot Noelle in the terminal at JFK airport.

Her arms are crossed over her chest, a glower twists her lips into a frown, and her big blue eyes—always brimming with sparkle and a hint of mischief—are narrowed in frustration.

Concern kicks behind my sternum as thoughts whip through my mind. Did she and her father have a falling out? Did something else happen at Primrose Sweets?

"Beautiful girl." I release my suitcase to grip her hips, pulling her against my chest and wrapping my arms around her, just needing to hug her when she looks this angry and miserable.

Shit. Is she upset with *me*?

She lets me hold her for a long moment before she steps back. She wipes her cheeks with her fingers before running them over her bouncy curls. Clearing her throat, she fixes me with a stern look. "Did you buy a hockey team in Tennessee?"

Fuck. The second she murmurs the question is the second

I realize how dirty Rick is going to play to keep me from having a relationship with his daughter. I don't know how he spun this tale to her, or what he said about me in the process, but I manage to tamp down my anger. At least, for the moment. Because spouting off to a hurt and angry Noelle in the middle of the arrivals hall days before Christmas isn't going to end well for anyone.

Pinching the bridge of my nose, I take a deep breath.

"Why didn't you tell me?" Her voice is strangled with tears she's unwilling to shed.

Double fuck.

"Is that when you went to Tennessee? Scott, that was over a week ago. I thought, shit, I thought we were…"

"What?" I ask, wanting her to finish that thought. What did she think about us? Because it suddenly feels like I've been more forthcoming about the future than she has. My hands curl into fists at the damage control I need to do now all thanks to her father.

"It doesn't matter."

"I didn't buy a hockey team."

"What?" Her eyes widen, disbelief still coloring her irises.

"Beautiful girl, do you really think I'd buy a hockey team and not tell you?" I ask, both hurt and insulted that after everything, she'd think me capable of being so flippant with the future I thought we were planning. Together.

She shakes her head uncertainly, her eyes wary, unreadable.

"Come on." I place my hand in the center of her spine and usher her toward the airport exit. "Let's grab a drink. Or lunch. Are you hungry?"

She nods, swiping at her nose. While she doesn't pull away from me, her body is tense and doesn't melt into mine the way I've come to expect. Clearly, there is tension between us and while I know some of it is because of our busy schedules over the past few weeks, I also know Rick and his big mouth escalated things.

Noelle indicates the car waiting for us and slides into the back seat. I exchange a few pleasantries with the driver, stow my suitcase in the trunk, and slip in beside her.

She's tense, biting her fingernails, her gaze trained out the window.

"What's happening here, Noelle?" I ask gently, but my patience is starting to fray. I just got off a freaking flight from California, after watching the Hawks lose in the third period, to be with my girl. And she's looking at me like she's unsure if she wants to spend Christmas with me at her side.

Again, I pinch the bridge of my nose, trying to put myself in her shoes but, shit, sometimes can't she see things from my perspective too? Can't she realize that it's not just her putting in effort to make this work, but I'm also giving my best?

"Tell me about Tennessee." She looks at me, her eyes still uncertain which pisses me off.

I heave out a sigh, glancing at the driver who respectfully pops in headphones and turns up the volume. Discreet guy; I can tell why Rick hired him.

"This is still under wraps; it hasn't been announced yet, but I've wanted to tell you for weeks."

She nods.

"Noah Scotch is retiring after this season."

Noelle sucks in an inhale, surprised, the same way most of the country will be. Hawks fans will be gutted but—"He wants to spend more time with his family. His knee isn't healing the way we hoped and…he's just…"

"Ready for the next chapter," Noelle supplies. "Indy's having another baby and his priorities have changed."

"Exactly."

"Are you upset?" Her tone is more curious than wary now, so I respond honestly.

"Sad to see him go, of course. Not just because he's a talented player and a strong leader but because he's become a...friend. But I respect the hell out of him for it too. I've watched guys destroy their home lives, ruin whatever good they had going on with their wives, kids, because of the game. Scotch is making the right call for his family and there's nothing more manly than that."

"I think so too."

I dip my chin in understanding. "Anyway, he and Jemmy Merrick—"

"Indy's dad."

"Yeah. They kicked around the idea of buying the Tennessee Thunderbolts. The Bolts have had over a decade of losses, haven't made it to the play-offs in nearly twenty years. The team, the entire franchise, needs to be rebuilt. It's a hell of a lot of work but it also means the price is more...doable."

Noelle arches a questioning eyebrow. "The two of them bought it outright?"

I shake my head and watch as the light in her eyes fades. I know she thinks I've kicked in money for it. She thinks I'm taking off more than I can chew or more than *we* can handle but, "Torsten and Rielle Hansen, along with Torst's brother and family, backed most of the sale. They'll be majority share-holders, with Jemmy and Noah having a smaller percentage. But Jemmy and Noah want to coach, and the arrangement worked well for all of them."

"Then why did you go?"

I breathe out a chuckle. "Because Noah asked me to. The Bolts former owner, Buck, and I go way, way back. He and my dad were friends and I've known him nearly my whole life. The fact that Noah came to me at all was gratifying. I wanted to help him, and I wanted to look out for Buck too. Make sure everyone felt the deal was fair, make sure it all went through without a hitch."

"Scotch respects you."

"And I admire him," I say easily.

She shakes her head, rubbing her fingers over her lips. Lips I want to kiss and coax and taste to remind her how damn good things are between us when her dad isn't mucking shit up. "Why the hell did my dad and Ben make it—"

"Ben?" I cut her off, knowing she means Tully. Fucking Rick.

Her expression tightens. "He was at dinner yesterday."

"The dinner you were looking forward to with your dad?" I can't hide the bite in my tone and Noelle hears it because she turns to look out the window again. "Why the hell did Rick bring him along?" I ask the question out of frustration, even though I know the answer. Scoffing, I spit out, "When are you going to make him respect you and your choices?"

Her head whips around. "He's my father, Scott."

"You're an adult, Noelle," I remind her.

She rolls her eyes, disproving my point.

"What happened with Ben?" I demand, hating that he probably pressed his slobbery mouth against Noelle's smooth cheek and tried to fucking chat her up over overpriced wine the fucker doesn't understand enough to appreciate.

"Nothing."

I lift my eyebrows and she squirms.

"He just makes me…uncomfortable. And I wish Dad hadn't invited him. Even Miguel—"

"Miguel?"

She smirks. "The host. I've known him my whole life. And even he was annoyed Ben was there."

"Intuitive guy." I narrow my eyes, waiting for the rest of the story.

"Dad wants me to work with Ben in the New Year on some marketing outreach, fresh ideas to generate more buzz about the Sharks. Throw weight behind Mike and see about endorsements that will propel him, and the team, to new heights in the city. Ben thinks—"

"I don't give a fuck about what Ben thinks," I snap, finally voicing my frustration with the situation. "What did you tell your dad? How are you going to work on marketing or PR with *Ben* when you're running two bakeries? We've barely spoken in two days since you were so busy closing up Primrose Boston and putting out fires at Primrose New York that—"

"You've been busy too," she says, more accusatory than I care for. "Flying off to Tennessee—"

"I'm sorry about the dinner. I thought—"

"It was the third time you cancelled on me. Then, before we can talk about it, you're dashing off to Los Angeles."

"We had a game!"

"And I have a business to run."

"Exactly." I lower my voice. "You have a business to run. Is that Primrose Sweets or the New York Sharks?"

"You know it's the bakery. I'm going to talk to my dad."

"When?" I press. "Because I'm not interested in Rick's head games. And frankly, you shouldn't be tolerating his shit either."

She closes her eyes for a long beat and when she opens them, the resignation that burns there hurts me. "Look, I just want to get through Christmas—"

I wince at the expression. Are we there already? To tolerating holidays instead of enjoying them? And didn't I voice something similar just last week?

"And then I'll talk to my dad," she murmurs.

"Okay," I say reluctantly.

When Noelle turns to look out her window, I do the same. The exhaustion of the game, of the flight, of the busiest time of the year, catches up to me and I close my eyes.

For the past five hours, all I could think about was getting here to be with my girl. I made it, and yet the relief I expected at seeing her never came. Because instead of the expected excitement, I'm filled with disappointment.

For Rick. For Ben. And, most unsettling, for Noelle.

AFTER A SHOWER AND A DRINK, I feel better. I think Noelle does too because she offers me a tentative smile as I enter the study, my hair still damp.

"Hey," she says, tucking her finger in the book she's reading to mark her place.

"What are you reading?" I take a seat on the chair across from her. The large windows give a glimpse of the cityscape and I take a moment to appreciate the beautiful view.

When I look back, Noelle is holding up the title for me.

I grin. *"Tender Is the Night."*

"I love F. Scott Fitzgerald. I read it every Christmas."

"You know I was named after him."

"What?" She laughs, placing the book down on a side table and sitting up straighter. "I figured you were named after your dad or grandfather or something."

"Nope. My Dad was William and my grandfather George."

She chuckles, eyeing me skeptically. "Why F. Scott Fitzgerald?"

"He had this quote," I pause, recalling it. "'I'm not sure what I'll do, but—well, I want to go places and see people. I want my mind to grow. I want to live where things happen on a big scale.' Mom read that and it stuck with her. Said if that's not the essence of what it's all about, going places, seeing people, growing your mind…what is?" I shrug. "I always liked the quote too. It's a good life motto."

"You've lived up to it."

"I hope so," I tell her truthfully.

She shifts in her chair again. "I'm sorry for arguing with you earlier."

"It's okay."

"No." She shakes her head. "I just, I always fall back into this pattern when I'm home. Doing what Daddy says, being the dutiful daughter. I don't want to disappoint him. For years, it was just the two of us and…I don't know what kind of relationship we'll have if it's not the one he designed for us."

"Don't you want to find out?" I ask gently.

She shakes her head, her eyes filling with moisture. "No. Because I'm worried it won't be one I like. Or want."

"Beautiful girl," I sigh, moving to her side and wrapping an arm around her shoulder. "You're not giving him enough credit." It's hard as fuck to say the words but I think they're true. If there is one person in this world Rick DiSanto loves, it's his daughter.

Noelle laughs and it holds a sarcastic edge, as if she knows how tough that sentiment was to share. But in her next breath, her tone is somber. "What if it's not enough?"

"What?"

She glances up at me and I get the distinct feeling we're not talking about just Rick anymore. "Love."

"Why wouldn't it be?"

She shrugs. "You've seen it, haven't you? Couples you thought couldn't breathe without each other and then, a few years in, reality, life, divorce papers…"

"I've seen it," I whisper, tightening my hold on her. "But I've also seen couples work through really hard times and come out stronger on the other side."

She raises a skeptical brow. "Like who?"

"My parents."

"Oh."

I kiss the top of her head. "We can figure this out, Noelle.

We just have to…communicate. Work together. We have to be on the same team."

"Yeah, of course," she murmurs, but she doesn't sound as convinced as I feel.

And that disappoints me too.

CHAPTER 21
NOELLE

I can't shake the unease that settles over my skin like an itchy sweater. Now that Scott is here, nothing is unfolding the way I thought it would. When we were in New Orleans, inviting him home for Christmas seemed like my best idea. Wrapped up in tinsel and inky skies and a sense of freedom, it filled me with giddiness.

But now that I'm back, in Dad's house, Scott's presence is more stress than salve. Will he and Dad get along? Will he be annoyed if I dip out to check on the bakery, leaving him with Dad? Will the tension that permeates the house like a draft, ease?

"I thought you were excited about dinner tonight?" Scott asks me as we dress for Christmas Eve dinner.

"I was. Am," I fumble the words.

He pierces me with a look.

"What?" I ask, annoyance in my tone as I shift into a defensive position. I understand Scott's look. He's wondering why the hell I'm on edge. He's thinking why is she unsettled in her family home. He's trying to figure out if it's him, making me respond this way, or if I'm always like this when I'm in New York.

And I don't want to admit that it's a combination of both. That I always feel mounting pressure when I enter my father's space. That I don't know how to shut down Dad's talk of legacy in support of my own business goals. That when I'm here, I revert to old habits, losing bits of the confidence that took me years to hone.

And that Scott being here is making it all glaringly obvious.

"Nothing," he murmurs, looking away.

My chest tightens as I roll my shoulders back when I really want to curl inwards. Somehow, his dismissal is worse than sharp words.

"Say what you mean," I mutter, half looking for a fight.

He tips his head at me, the corner of his mouth twitching. He's got a pulse on me which he makes obvious when he states, rather than asks, "What do you want from me, Noelle?"

I swipe my hands over my face, suddenly feeling like I'm going to cry. Angry tears burn the back of my nose, frustrated tears swell in the corners of my eyes, and disappointed tears gather at the base of my throat.

"I don't know," I whisper.

Hurt blazes across Scott's expression, making me feel worse. But at least I was honest, right?

"Well, I suggest you figure it out soon," he says in a clipped tone. Fixing his sweater, he leaves me alone in my bathroom, closing the door behind him.

I sink down on the closed toilet seat and close my eyes, willing myself not to cry. I'll mess up my makeup and any tears will only fuel Dad's dismissal of Scott, a rejection of the relationship I thought we were building.

Jesus. I take a few deep inhales, calming my warring emotions. When I feel steady enough, I stand, finish getting ready, and go downstairs to the formal dining room for dinner.

Except when I enter the room, I freeze. Because Ben fucking Tully is seated at one end of the table, with Dad at the other, and in between them, a grimacing Scott.

Shit.

All three men stand when I enter the room. I paste a smile on my face. "Merry Christmas."

Ben scurries forward, leaning into me to kiss my cheek. "Merry Christmas, Noelle. You look beautiful."

"Doesn't she?" Dad beams at me, feigning like nothing's wrong when this is clearly going to be the most awkward Christmas Eve dinner ever. "Ben was going to be alone for the holidays. I said, absolutely not, you'll celebrate with us. Isn't that right, Noelle?" He embellishes, reading the unasked questions swirling in my mind.

"Of course," I say, my throat dry.

I swear I hear Scott scoff, a quiet sound, quiet enough that I'm not sure if I'm imagining it. I turn pleading eyes on him, but his expression is stone, his eyes unreadable. Shit, shit, shit.

I slip into my chair, with Dad and Ben on either side, and Scott across from me. By the pinch between his eyebrows, I know he's frustrated. Hell, I'm frustrated too. But when I open my mouth, the voice in my head cuts me off. *Your father only wants what's best for you, Noelle.*

One of the kitchen staff, Izzy, appears to fill wine glasses and my heart lurches gratefully. She shoots me a sympathetic smile and pours a little extra in my glass.

"To family and hockey." Dad lifts his glass.

We all follow suit, but by the thin press of Scott's lips, I can tell that didn't go over well with him either. Feeling incredibly out of sorts, I take a huge mouthful, and begin to fill my plate with items from the massive antipasto assortment on the table: slices of mozzarella, Italian meats, crusty Italian bread. There's roasted red peppers and pitted cocktail olives, artichoke hearts and shrimp cocktail. I know better than to fill up on this, especially when there's various fish to eat and pasta to try, but I'd rather stuff my face than speak at this meal. Because anything I say is going to be misconstrued by one of the men present.

I keep my eyes trained on my plate as Dad and Ben talk, the conversation quickly sliding into hockey.

"When are you moving to Tennessee?" Ben asks Scott point-blank.

Scott shifts in his chair, reaching across the table to help himself to more cheese. "I'm not," he says easily.

"No?" Dad frowns, but I can tell by the way his eyes slide my way, that he's putting on a show. Dammit. "I could have sworn you were one of the new buyers for the Bolts. With your experience and—"

"You and I both know I didn't buy the team, Rick," Scott cuts him off.

Ben moves back in his seat, surprised by Scott's tone.

Dad lifts a mocking eyebrow. "We do? I was under the impression—"

"Scott, can you please pass the artichokes?" I cut in, trying to diffuse the building tension.

Dad and Scott both flip annoyed gazes my way.

"I bet you're excited to take on more of a leadership role, Noelle," Ben says, either completely oblivious or catty as fuck. *Read the room, Ben.*

Dad settles back some and gives an approving nod. "She's going to jump right in. With the two of you working together, our new marketing campaigns will make waves through the city." He narrows his eyes at Scott. "Are you still working with Anderson Marketing?" he asks, tossing out the name of a Scottish-American marketing agency that's recently gained notoriety in the sports world for developing fresh, edgy campaigns.

Scott clears his throat. "Did you ask Noelle how she feels

about this new leadership role you're assuming she's going to do?"

Fuck. I hang my head. Why the hell is Scott throwing me under the bus? I feel the heavy stares of all three men on the crown of my head. When I force myself to meet their eyes, I internally wince. This is so not how I imagined Christmas going.

"Noelle, tell Scott how much you like being a Shark. A vital member of the franchise, a valued member of our family," Dad says, more demanding than encouraging.

While I know his use of *family* is meant to signify the Sharks family, by Scott's horrified expression, he interpreted it differently.

"Why wouldn't she want to work with me, Scott?" Ben quips. "She knows together, we'll be unstoppable. Right, sweetheart?"

Scott clenches his fork and knife so tightly, his knuckles pale. "Or," he throws down, "you can tell your father and Ben just how amazing things are going at Primrose Boston and—"

"Bah," Dad cuts in, flicking a dismissive hand, as if my bakery is nothing more than a passing whim. My angry, frustrated, disappointed tears are back, wreaking havoc on my facial expressions as I blink furiously. "Noelle knows where she's really needed, where she can make an impact. And it's not making cupcakes for four-year-old birthday parties."

Ouch. That lands like a jab to the chest.

"That's what you think she does?" Scott jumps to my defense and my gratitude spikes even as I roll my lips closed. "Rick, Noelle is a smart and savvy businesswoman. It's not easy running two bakeries, in two different cities, in a handful of years. She's expanding her brand, growing her business, and gaining popularity. Her social media—"

Dad turns toward me, again dismissing Scott. He lifts his eyebrows. "Is that true? Are you going to abandon your legacy, everything I've worked for, and turn your back on us to make frosting?"

"Rick…" Ben's voice is soft, and he trails off.

My mouth opens and closes several times, but no words come out. I feel the frustration, the challenge, rolling off Scott's shoulders, crashing down on me, from across the table. He's waiting for me to stand up for myself, to use my voice, to be honest with my father.

"Well?" Dad asks, crossing his arms over his chest. He waits me out, the way he has since I was a little girl, knowing I would come around to his way of thinking, to his decision, to him.

Obey your father, Noelle. God, I wish my mother was here. Would she still ask me to defer to him? Or, now that I'm grown, would she advocate on my behalf? I'll never know and the realization causes my chest to ache.

With every second that ticks by, Scott's disappointment, his hurt presses down on me.

"Daddy," I finally mutter, my voice cracking.

Dad stares at me and after a long, awkward, awful moment, he turns back to Scott. "Guess you don't know my daughter as well as you think, Reland."

And Scott is done. He tosses down his napkin and slides his chair back. "Guess not," he mutters, glancing around the table. "I think I should go. You'll enjoy your meal more without me—"

"No." I shoot up in my chair. "Wait, Scott, I…" I scurry around to his side of the table. "Wait." I reach for his hand.

He lets me catch his fingers. He stands still and stares at me, waiting for me to say something, anything. But under my Dad's and Ben's gazes, I falter, again. In this moment, I can't stand myself and still, I can't bring myself to say the words that should be said.

Stay. I'm sorry. Thank you. I love you.

Scott brushes a kiss over my cheek. "Merry Christmas, Noelle."

Then he turns on his heel and walks away from me. From us.

And I let him go.

"Told you, honey," Dad mutters as I sit back down. "He was never in for the right reasons."

"Don't you want to be with a Shark anyway?" Ben wonders aloud.

I don't say anything, their callous words hurtful and real. When Izzy comes in to clear the appetizers, I excuse myself to check on Scott.

But when I enter my bedroom, his suitcase is gone. And I have no one to blame but myself.

Sinking to the edge of my bed, I finally let the tears come. They trail down my cheeks in slow motion, dripping off my chin and dotting the leather of my pants like raindrops.

I pick up my phone and tap out several texts to Scott.

NOELLE

Are you going back to Boston?

NOELLE

Can we talk?

NOELLE

I'm sorry that was tense. I'll talk to Dad.

But I don't send a single one. In the end, I call Averie and the second she answers, she knows.

"Oh, Noelle," my best friend whispers as I sob. "You're going to be okay. Everything is going to work out fine."

But how can it? When this time, it's all my fault.

"Why are you calling me?" Jayde answers.

I wince, pinching the bridge of my nose. Striding back and forth in front of the airline's check-in stand, I glance at the frustrated and frantic faces of Christmas travelers around me.

"This was a mistake," I mutter.

"What was?" Jayde's voice is gentler than I've ever heard it, and for the first time, I realize how invested my assistant is in my life. She genuinely wants me to be happy and the thought knocks me upside the head because I've never considered her a confidante, but the truth is…she's the one constant I've had for the past few years.

"I'm at the airport."

Jayde groans. "You told me to book your flight for the morning of the twenty-sixth."

"I know."

Jayde's quiet for a long moment. "What happened?"

"Rick DiSanto," I start, my voice rising which each word. "He invited Ben fucking Tully to dinner."

Jayde swears.

"And conned Noelle into going to dinner with him the other night."

"With Ben?" Jayde gasps.

"And Rick," I mutter, slowing my pace. I grip the back of my neck. "He lied to her."

"About?"

"Said I was buying the freaking Tennessee Thunderbolts when—"

"Oh my God! Is that why you went to Tennessee? Are you—"

"No!" Shit, I shouldn't have said a damn thing about it. "No. Listen, I was helping out a friend, that's all. But Rick knew that and spun something entirely different to Noelle."

"I'm sorry, Scott."

"Yeah, well, I'm at the goddamn airport. I need a flight to Boston," I say gruffly.

Silence ticks by for several seconds.

"Jayde?"

"Maybe you should go back and smooth things over with Noelle. It's Christmas and—"

"I don't pay you for your advice on my personal life."

She snorts. "Yes, you do. Scott, do you really want to leave things like this with Noelle?"

"Of course not." I resume my pacing. "But what am I supposed to do, Jayde? She's never shown much of an interest in my career, in my work. I've done nothing but support her and the expansion of her business. I'm still trying to do that," I state, recalling my upcoming meeting with the Huxley brothers. "And the first thing that comes up, related to my business, and she takes her father's side and accuses me of going behind her back to buy a goddamn NHL team."

"He's her father, Scott," Jayde says softly.

"Yeah. So above everyone else, he should support her and her dreams. Yet, from where I'm sitting, all he's done is try to sabotage her goals in favor of his own. She doesn't stick up for herself, Jayde. She didn't stick up for us." The last part comes out quieter, and once the words pierce the air, I realize the heart of it all. "Her silence tonight proves that I'm temporary. A fleeting moment in her life. That she's not as invested as I am."

I'm hurt because she didn't stick up for us. She doesn't have faith in *us*. If she did, she would know I would never buy a hockey team without talking to her first. If she did, she wouldn't keep pandering to her father's ridiculous bullshit.

"Scott—"

"Can you book me a flight?" I cut her off, resigned to my decision.

"Yeah, sure," Jayde agrees quietly. "I'll email you the details."

"I'll be at the bar." Then, realizing my error too late, I swear. "Shit, Jayde. It's Christmas Eve and—"

"It's fine."

"No, it's not. You're probably with—"

"I could use the fifteen-minute break from my family," she jokes.

"Thanks for…everything. Running my life." I head toward a pub in the corner of the airport.

"Someone has to," she quips back. "Merry Christmas, Scott."

"Merry Christmas." I disconnect the call as I settle onto a barstool.

The bartender takes one look at my face and pours two shots of vodka. He slides one across to me and picks up the other for himself.

"To next year," he murmurs.

I tip my head and raise my glass. Then, I toss it back, letting the clear liquor burn a path to my belly. One filled with frustration and regret.

Because I'm tired of waiting for next year. This was

supposed to be my year. This was supposed to be my time. With Noelle. We're supposed to be an us.

CHRISTMAS on my own is a depressing affair. When I FaceTime Mom and my family, I inject a cheery lightness into my tone that doesn't match the morose feelings swirling through my chest.

"You sure you're okay?" Mom asks quietly after my cousins have moved back to the kitchen. Their adorable children can be seen in the background, running around the kitchen island. As Mom moves away from the group, into a quiet sitting area, their joy fades from view. "What's going on, Scotty?"

I blow out a sigh, picking up my third coffee for the day. I'm going stir-crazy in my quiet house, jumpy on caffeine, irritated by the emptiness. "Nothing."

A small smile curls Mom's lips. "Even at forty-five—"

"Forty-four."

Her grin grows. "I can still read my son. What happened with Noelle?"

I sigh heavily. "I thought we were planning a future together, committing to something larger and..."

Mom purses her lips, widening her eyes at me to continue.

"And she thinks we're temporary."

"She told you that? Or you're reading that based off something that happened?"

"For seventy-three—"

"Seventy-two, thank you very much." Mom's eyes, the same bright green as mine, glimmer.

"You're still perceptive."

"As an eagle. What happened?"

Staring at Mom's face on the screen, I suddenly wish I didn't spend so many Christmases here, in a big house, alone. Not when I could have been with her and my aunt, my family, chasing toddlers around kitchen islands and dressing up as Santa.

"Scotty," Mom prods.

I open my mouth and the whole story tumbles out. The gala from over the summer, the rivalry with Rick, Primrose Sweets and the pop-up shop at The Meadows. I tell Mom more about New Orleans and Christmas ornaments, more about the woman with keen eyes and an infectious laugh, who already rules my heart. Then, about the Thunderbolts and Ben Tully and New York.

"And, she stayed in New York," I finish, unable to hide the resentment from my tone.

Mom watches me for a moment. "You love her."

"Of course, I love her."

Mom's smile is blinding now. "Good for you, Scott."

"Mom, she stayed in New York," I spell it out again.

"Well of course she did; it's her father."

I close my eyes and pinch the bridge of my nose. "Why the hell does everyone keep saying that?"

"Because it's true. Scotty, when you played that poker game and bet the Eagles—"

I groan but Mom continues, undeterred.

"You knew your father was going to be upset but you also knew, deep down, that he would forgive you. Support you. Encourage you to carve out space for your own dreams."

"We didn't talk for years," I remind her.

Mom shakes her head. "That was more your fault than his."

"What?" My neck snaps up at the insinuation in her tone.

"He was at your first game."

"He was?" I whisper.

"Of course, Scotty. Did you really think he wouldn't show

up for you?" Mom looks hurt by the thought and a lump gathers at the base of my throat.

An unfamiliar sensation, stinging, pricks the corners of my eyes and I drop my head. "No, I knew he would come around."

"Exactly," Mom says reassuringly. "Not everyone has that, Scotty. Not everyone knows with certainty that their decision, whether it be an amazing choice or a disastrous mistake, will be met with acceptance. Deep down, you knew. It sounds like Noelle may not and she's not ready to risk that."

Noelle's words flit through my mind. *I don't know what kind of relationship we'll have if it's not the one he designed for us.*

"Maybe," I reluctantly say.

"She may not ever be ready to risk that," Mom adds. I frown. "Or maybe she needs more time. Either way, she may not realize that you're still there for her with the way you left New York. If she doesn't have the ability to trust her father as a constant, what do you think your actions just showed her?" Mom's tone holds a hint of the scolding from my younger years. Even as her words hit me like a truth bomb, her tone is strangely comforting. Nostalgic.

And I realize… "You're right."

Mom dips her head, knowingly.

"So, what do I do?" I wonder aloud, even more agitated. With myself, with my actions, with the permeating quiet of being back in Boston. Alone.

Mom tilts her head. "You really don't know?"

I scoff.

"Something big, Scotty. Go big or—"

"Stay home," I say, finishing the words Dad always used to say. He changed the common "go big or go home" statement, arguing if you're not going to go all in, you may as well not leave home in the first place.

At the reminder, Mom chuckles and I join in.

"Thanks, Mom."

"Always," she replies. "Make your New Year's better than your Christmas, Scotty."

I huff out a laugh and nod. "Will do."

"And come visit me soon."

"Or you can come here," I offer, wondering if she doesn't visit much because I never extend an invite. To me, it's a given, but considering how busy the last few years have been, maybe Mom doesn't view it that way.

As her expression softens and emotion fills her eyes, I realize my error and a crushing guilt grips me. "I'd love to, Scott."

"Me too, Mom. I miss you. I'll see you soon."

"Hugs and kisses," Mom murmurs, another throwback from my childhood.

"Hugs and kisses," I repeat.

When I disconnect the call, I collapse on the sofa in my living room and close my eyes.

Shit, I messed this up. Big time. Mom was right. While I thought I was showing up for Noelle, consistently investing in her dreams and wanting to be part of her future, I bolted at our first disagreement. I can't blame her for losing confidence in us, for questioning her trust in me. Even though Rick sucks at supporting her dreams, he always shows up. He's always there.

If I want to be with Noelle, I have to show her that I have her back no matter what. Even if she chooses to believe her father's bullshit. Even if she played nice with Ben Tully for Rick's sake. Even if I don't like it; I love her more.

And I need to prove that.

As an idea forms in my head, I snicker, shaking my head. I stare at the empty space in the corner of the living room where a Christmas tree should be. One decorated with Waterford crystal ornaments and travel memories.

Next year, I resolve.

Next year will be different. Better.

CHAPTER 23
NOELLE

"Told you so." Dad shakes his head after Izzy closes the door behind Ben. "Reland was always up to something. Right from the beginning. Now that you're back in New York, I think it's pretty obvious, you should be with a man like Ben. Someone who can handle running the Sharks. Someone who wants to be part of this family, this team." Dad sits back down at the table and refills our wine glasses. "We can go over a few things for the new marketing tomorrow morning and then—"

"Tomorrow's Christmas," I murmur.

"Huh?" Dad settles back in his chair, his wine glass in hand.

"Tomorrow is Christmas," I say, clearly.

"Exactly. We can get a jump-start on things since everyone else will be taking the day off. I flagged a few concepts I want your opinion on."

I stare at him, almost as if seeing him for the first time even though parts of my heart have known the truth for so long. Dad is a workaholic. Work, business, comes before everything else. Even Christmas. Even my happiness.

Is that why Mom always encouraged me to obey him? Because it was easier than fighting a constant uphill battle? Did she ever feel the way I do right now? Helpless and resigned.

"Why did you lie about Scott and the Thunderbolts?" I question, leaning back in my chair, wine glass also in hand. My gaze meets his, steely blue versus icy gray.

"I, I heard that—"

"Why'd you lie, Dad?"

He rubs his palm along his chin, his cheeks growing splotchy with frustration. Dad doesn't like being called out and since everyone knows it, most people back down. Right now, it's clear I've been backing down for too long. So I cling to the stubbornness I inherited from him and wait him out.

"Honey, Scott Reland is forty-four years—"

"I know how old he is, Daddy. What I don't know is why you keep pushing Ben on me, why you lied to me about Scott buying the Thunderbolts, and why you don't care about Primrose Sweets the same way I've always cared and supported your dedication to the Sharks."

Dad's eyes narrow as he stares me down. After a long minute he swears. Then sighs. "Sometimes you're just like your mother."

I rear back, surprised. "What? I assumed I got my stubbornness from you."

Dad chuckles. "Stubbornness, yes. But assertiveness and loyalty, that's all Rose." He pauses, then sighs, "You and I both know I'm not diplomatic." His tone holds a note of apology.

I nod in agreement, my jaw set.

"You're angry with me."

"Yes."

Dad sighs heavily, gulping half the contents of his wine glass. "I don't like Reland."

"You don't know him."

"You can do better."

"Then Ben? I agree," I spit back, emboldened by Dad's comparing me to Mom. For years, I assumed I got my business sense, my ambition to prove myself from him but… knowing I've got some of mom's characteristics fuels me to stand up for myself. I wish I did it hours ago, when Scott was here, but the truth is, I'm doing it for me more than him. For the life I want. For the part of an us I'd like to grow into. "It's time."

Dad frowns. "What is?"

"I need you to hear me, really hear me, when I say I'm not interested in taking over the Sharks."

"Noelle, don't be rash. I know you're frustrated but—"

"I'm not. Frustrated, I mean. I'm being honest. My heart, everything I want for my future, is with Primrose Sweets. I'm doubling down on that, Dad. This isn't a phase. I don't want the Sharks as some backup plan or safety net. I don't want that life."

"What do you think you'd have with Reland?" Dad sputters back, grasping at straws.

"A big love," I say, realizing how true the words are. "Breakfast beignets and colorful Christmas ornaments," I murmur.

"Huh?" Dad's eyes widen. "Noelle DiSanto, you're smarter than this. Everything with Reland was fun and exciting because it was new. You were moved by the novelty of it. He's young, flashy, wealthy, and—"

"You're joking, right?" I cut him off as my annoyance flairs. "I'm young, flashy, and wealthy too."

He opens and closes his mouth several times.

"Scott supports me." I rattle off about the pop-up shop and the bakery.

"Really?" Dad places his wine glass down to fold his arms across his chest. "Then where is he?"

"Home," I state, standing from the table and pushing in my chair. "I'm going back to Boston. I—"

"Now wait a minute," Dad cuts me off, clamoring to his feet. When he realizes I'm serious, awareness followed by a strange acceptance fills his expression. "Stay."

"Dad."

"Please. Stay and let's have Christmas. We'll talk. About your bakery. And the pop-up shop. We'll…figure things out."

I shift from one foot to the other, wondering if this is a sincere olive branch or if Dad is going to try to wrangle me into the Sharks fold if a I give an inch.

"Please, Noelle. I'm asking you." At the sincerity in his tone, I fall back.

"Okay. But no working on Christmas."

Dad opens his arms and I fall into them, closing my eyes as he hugs me tight. "Promise," he agrees.

"STOP LOOKING AT YOUR PHONE," Averie advises me on the morning of the twenty-sixth. "Although, I don't blame you. I can't believe he hasn't called yet either."

I blow out a sigh, swinging my legs from my perch on the table in the bakery kitchen. "It's been two days."

"But who's counting?" Averie tightens the bun at the top of her head.

I scowl. "Don't be flippant. This is…serious."

My best friend leans against the table opposite mine and crosses her arms over her chest. "Have you reached out to him?"

"No." I sulk.

"Why not?"

"He left my house, just up and left, Christmas Eve dinner," I remind her.

"After sticking up for you and your goals. He took on Papa DiSanto," Averie points out.

I chew the corner of my mouth, looking away.

"What'd your dad say?" Averie asks gently.

"You mean after 'I told you so'?"

She winces. "Yeah."

I sigh. "After Ben—"

Averie pretends to vomit, complete with big, bugged-out eyes and gagging sounds.

"Left," I carry on, "I finally stuck up for myself with Dad. I told him I'm not going to take on anything with the Sharks because I'm going all in on Primrose. On my dreams."

"Finally!" Averie shrieks. "Jesus, I've been waiting years for you to grow a—"

"Backbone. I know."

"I was going to say a set, but sure, backbone works."

I flip her the middle finger and she laughs. "We had words and then…a really great Christmas Day. I think when he realized how serious I was about leaving Christmas Eve and flying to be with Scott, it was like a wake-up call. I was surprised when he asked me to stay, skeptical even, but I'm glad I did. We spent Christmas together and…really talked. The way we should have been doing for years." I smile. "I think my mom would have been happy."

"Good. I'm happy for you, girl. You know I always want the best for you, but Papa DiSanto withholding his support sucked."

"Yeah," I agree.

"And Scott was nothing but supportive from day one."

"I know," I lament.

"So I think you got your answer."

"What's that?" I peer up at Averie, waiting for some guidance.

"Phone's work both ways," she says easily, straightening. "Now help me get started. We're going to get slammed this week for New Year's parties and I miss baking with you."

I hop off the table and wrap Averie in a hug. "I miss you too. And thank you."

"You got this, DiSanto. Nobody's going to show up for you if you don't show up for yourself. This time, it's gotta be you."

Ah, there's the wisdom I was waiting for. Knowing what I need to do, I hug Averie tighter. "You're right."

SNOW BLANKETS the ground in soft lulls and waves when the plane lands in Boston. As the door opens and the passengers begin to exit into the terminal, I pull my scarf tighter and shiver against the cold.

Still, as I collect my suitcase and step into the freezing, snowy morning air, I grin up at the gray sky. Because it's now home. "Good to be back," I mutter to myself as I wait in the taxi line.

Instead of going home, I head straight to Primrose Sweets. As I enter the space, I breathe in the cinnamon and sugar that seems to hang in the air, urging me forward.

This is your dream. This is your goal. This is your life.

The space whispers around me, coming to life. I discovered my passion young. I found my home by accident. The only thing missing is the man of my dreams and it's because I pushed him away. I didn't make him feel like a priority, the way he tried to make me feel.

I pull out a mixing bowl, some flour and sugar. I whistle to myself as I gather eggs and cinnamon and vanilla extract.

Then, I dig through a cupboard for the secret ingredient. When I discover the dried cranberries, I grin.

Going home to New York, seeing Dad, messing everything up with Scott, reminded me of the future I truly want.

One where I'm happy. And Scott makes me happy.

"Yeah, that's it. I just got the email," I confirm, scanning the document. "All looks good. Yep, can you courier that over? Great, thanks. Appreciate your help with this. Take care."

I place down my phone, still peering at the document, when the doorbell rings. I pause, and glance over my shoulder, wondering if it's a delivery or if Jayde has finally taken pity on me and decided to show up and annoy me into a better mood.

The bell rings again and I close the top of my laptop, moving to answer it.

I pull the door wide open and freeze, staring into the sparkling, hopeful, blazing blue eyes of, "Noelle."

"Hey, Scotty," she murmurs, licking her lips nervously.

"Come in." I hold the door wide, a gust of cold snapping against us.

Noelle scurries inside, her hands clutching a cake box. She stands on the weather mat in front of the door and gazes up at me, her unruly curls kept in check by the hat tugged down to her ears. "This is for you." She thrusts the cake box into my hands.

"Wait, what? What are you doing here?"

At the coolness in my tone, she shuffles back a step, her eyes darting to the floor.

"Noelle." I balance the cake box in one hand, reaching out to touch her shoulder with the other.

"I should have called," she murmurs, not meeting my gaze.

"What? No. I'm glad you're here. To see you. I…" I fumble my words, unsure what to say, how to apologize. I have a whole plan but I'm still working through things in my head and now she's here and…I don't want to mess it up again.

"I'm sorry," she says the words clearly, directly, like an announcement. Her eyes slam into mine, brimming with regret and apology and…a shimmer of the love I want to lose myself in. "I should have stood up to my father. I—"

"No, no." I shake my head. "I understand why you didn't. I pushed you and—"

"You were so much more honest than I was. You deserve so much more than I gave you, but—"

"You're perfect. And I'm in—"

"I love you, Scott."

We both pause, breathless and starry-eyed and chilly from standing so close to the door.

"I love you. I want you. And I'm sor—"

I pull her into me, wrapping one arm around her back fiercely, while trying to balance the cake box on my open palm. Before she can apologize again, I press my mouth to hers, swallowing her regret and kissing her with my forgiveness. "I'm sorry too," I murmur against her mouth. "I'm so fucking sorry and I'm so fucking in love with you."

She hangs onto my hips, tucking her fingers into the waistband of my jeans as she looks up at me. "I'm relieved to hear it."

"You think feelings can change that quickly?"

She shrugs. "It's hard for me to trust this sometimes." She

gestures between us. "Averie pointed out I've never had to work to make a relationship work and I think she was right. But I want to work with you, Scotty. I made you a cake."

"A cake?" I glance at the box in my hand.

She nods, pulling her hat off her head, her curls springing wildly. "A carrot cake. With—"

"Cranberries," I say, glancing down at the cake after gently lifting the lid. "Like—"

"Your grandmother. I know we're supposed to start new traditions but part of the reason we click, part of why we understand each other so well, is because of our pasts. The lifestyle, the hockey world, we're both a part of. I tried so hard to resist it but in doing so, I was resisting you and, Scotty, I want you. I want a life, a future, with you."

"Even with the hockey?" I add hopefully.

"Definitely with the hockey because it's part of your life. And I love you. And your childhood memories and traditions and everything that makes you happy."

Her words cause a ball of emotion to travel up my throat. I choke out a sound, half laugh, half sob, as I look from the beautiful cake to Noelle's breathtaking face. "Come have cake with me?"

"Always." She shrugs out of her winter parka and slips her arm through mine.

We enter my kitchen and automatically, the chill that hung in the air seems to evaporate. The loneliness, the quiet, the depressing emptiness transforms into a warm glow I want to live in.

Without saying a word, Noelle makes us two lattes while I get cake plates and a knife and forks. When we're seated at the kitchen island, we smile at each other over the carrot cake she made for us.

"We need to communicate better," I tell her.

"I know. I spoke to my dad."

I pause from cutting the cake. "And?"

"And I'm going all in on Primrose. I told him I don't want a future, career wise, with the Sharks. It seems like he finally understood."

I smile at Noelle, reaching for her hand. "He did; he told me as much."

She rears back, surprised. "You spoke to my dad?"

I nod, cutting her a slice of cake. I place it in front of her, passing her a fork. "I did."

"When?"

"Yesterday."

"Why?" she wonders.

"That's a good question." I sit on the barstool next to her and chuckle, shifting awkwardly. "I wanted to apologize for how I acted on Christmas Eve."

"You did?"

"Yeah, not my finest moment. But I also wanted him to know that you're amazing and thoughtful and ambitious. And that he's the guy who always has and should show up for you…and he needs to show you that, no matter what your future looks like."

She laughs, her eyes wide. "You went to bat for me."

"I'll always go to bat for you. I just didn't show you that the way I should have."

"Yes, you did," she argues.

"No." I shake my head. "I shouldn't have cancelled our dinner and flown to Tennessee without having a conversation with you first. I shouldn't have left on Christmas Eve. I should have done a lot of things differently, but Noelle, beautiful girl, if you give me another shot, I want to make it up to you. I want to prove that I can be a man, *the* man, you can count on. No matter what."

"Yes," she says with no hesitation.

"Yes?"

She nods, reaching for my fingers and squeezing. "And I promise to be more supportive, to show up and show interest in the Hawks, in your career. I want us to communicate better, to not only have late nights and early mornings but midday lunches and phone conversations. I want to build a life with you, Scott."

"Yes," I say immediately. "I want that too."

"Then let's eat cake."

"Let's eat cake, beautiful."

I dig into my piece and the moment I taste the carrot cake, I moan appreciatively, my eyes closing. For a second, I'm transported back to my childhood. To a full table on Christmas morning, to my grandmother's laughter, to Dad's smart-ass quips, and my aunt's long-winded stories. I remember my childhood and realize that the loneliness and emptiness I experienced as an adult is a result of my choices instead of everyone else's.

Needing to take responsibility for that, I blurt out, "Want to meet my mom?"

Noelle's face glows. "I'd love to."

"When was the last time you went to Seattle?"

"It's been a minute," she admits, her look questioning.

"How do you feel about ringing in the new year there?"

"With your mom?"

"And aunt, my cousins, and their kids."

Noelle grins. "So, a big, rowdy, overwhelming family gathering."

"Exactly," I say, wondering if it will be too much, too soon.

"Yes," she says easily. "Yes, let's do it."

Then she leans forward and kisses me hard, and I breathe in cinnamon, sugar, and pure love.

CHAPTER 25
NOELLE

I t's early when I wake the following morning. The sky is a grayish-white, casting Scott's living room in a cool, almost ethereal glow. I make myself a latte and settle onto the living room sofa, staring out at the expansive property, coated with snow.

Scott's still sleeping and knowing how rarely he sleeps in, the sounds of his light snoring cause me to giggle. I take my first sip of coffee, savoring the boldness of the espresso beans, and close my eyes.

This is the life I want. One where I wake up with Scott, excited to start the day. Of course, there are things we need to talk through and figure out. But knowing that we both want to do that, that we're both ready to put in the time and work, the necessary communication, to make that happen fills me with a certainty I haven't felt in years.

The buzzing of my phone causes the peaceful feeling flooding my chest to tighten. The only person who would call me this early is Dad. Or Averie, but I'm really praying there isn't another disaster at the bakery.

I glance at my phone on the coffee table. When I read

Dad's name, a hint of indecision flickers through my mind before I squash it and answer the call.

"Hi, Dad."

"Hey, honey." His tone is softer than usual, a thread of regret present. "How was your flight?"

"Fine, thanks. You're up early."

He sighs. "Couldn't sleep."

I frown. It's very unlike Dad to admit when anything is amiss in his personal life. "What's going on?" I tighten my grip on the phone, expecting the barrage of Sharks issues he's going to wrangle me into helping with. Public relations events, a charity gala, a well-placed press release, something is coming, and I hold my breath, waiting for the obligation with a slice of pain to hit me.

"Scott called me," he says gruffly.

"Yeah," my voice wavers. Where is he going with this? Is he going to forbid me from dating Scott? Or try to?

"He told you?"

"Just that you spoke. Not really what you spoke about…"

"Yeah. Well, it was…eye-opening."

I close my eyes, a bundle of nerves zinging through my limbs.

"I'm sorry, Noelle." Dad's voice is so heavy with sincerity and regret, my eyes pop open.

"I, wh-what?" I sputter, confused. What the hell did Scott say?

"I never listened or trusted you the way I should have. The way you proved to me I could. I was so stuck on my own ideas, on my beliefs of what was best, that I never considered it may not be what's *right* for you. Starting a business in New York isn't easy, expanding a business and seeing growth is damn near impossible, and you've done both in a handful of years. You pulled it off, kid, and we never celebrated it the way we should've. The way I should've. I'm so damn sorry."

Unexpected tears collect in the corners of my eyes. I roll

my lips together, pressing my mouth closed tightly to try to stem the emotions welling inside of me.

"Noelle?" Dad asks after a long second.

"Thank you." My voice breaks and Dad swears, finally realizing just how much his lack of support hurt, cut, all these years.

Dad clears his throat as we both collect ourselves. He's never been comfortable with big feelings, with messy moments, and right now, we're both overwhelmed with them. "I want to ask you for a favor."

I freeze, closing my eyes. My heart skips a beat. Was he just trying to butter me up so I can't say no to his next demand?

"I'd like for you to open a pop-up shop at the arena here, in New York. If you'd like, I mean."

My eyes fly open, and I gasp. "Wait, what?"

"It's long overdue, honey. I should've been your first arena. Not The Meadows. Will you do it?"

"Oh my God. Yes. Of course," I laugh out, a new rush of emotion coursing through me. "I'd love to. Thank you, Daddy."

"Don't thank me. You earned it. A long, long time ago. But, uh, no Hawks colors here, okay?"

I snort. "Just red and black," I promise, mentioning the Sharks colors.

"Red and black," Dad repeats. "So, uh, how are things? With Reland, I mean."

"They're…pretty great."

Dad's quiet and I can hear his thoughts turning over in his head. Moments tick by as he comes to terms with what I'm really saying. *Scott isn't going anywhere.*

"I love him, Daddy."

"Yeah. Well, he loves you too." The certainty with which he says the words makes me smile. Dads know these things, and mine would be the last to admit it if it wasn't true.

"There's not much more a dad can hope for than that. I uh, I'd like to take you both to dinner the next time you come to the city."

I nod, knowing how hard this is for him, recognizing how hard he's trying. "We'd love that."

"Good, good. Okay then, honey, I need to get to the office."

"Of course," I say, straining to listen for Scott's light snoring. Instead, I hear the running water of the shower and know he's awake.

"I'll email you some details for the pop-up shop and, well, we're ready when you are, Noelle."

"Thanks, Daddy. I hope, I hope it's a success."

"It will be."

I chuckle. "How can you be so sure?"

"You're a DiSanto, Noelle. And we don't put our names on anything less than our best. Your best is more than enough, honey. It always has been."

"I love you, Dad."

"Love you too. Say, um, hello to Reland—Scott—for me."

"I will. 'Bye, Dad."

I disconnect the call but remain curled up by the big bay window, admiring the snowflakes that stream from the sky.

A swell of happiness, a dash of giddiness, an overwhelming sense of freedom, like the future, all the tomorrows belong entirely to me, jolts through me, stronger than espresso. I guess they always have but right now, it *feels* like it.

"Good morning, beautiful," Scott says as he enters the room. A pair of joggers hang low on his hips, a plain T-shirt sculpting to his strong chest and biceps.

"Morning, Scotty." I tip my face up as he approaches and wastes no time kissing me. I shift on the couch, my knees widening to accommodate his frame as he drops to his knees, his arms snaking around my waist. We're nearly eye level and he smiles, taking my breath away. "How'd you sleep?"

"Better with you in my bed."

I grin. "Me too."

"Good. All okay?" He tips his head toward my phone.

"Yes, better than good. That was my dad."

Scott lifts an eyebrow before he dips his head and presses a kiss to my collarbone.

"He asked if I'd like a pop-up stand at the arena in New York."

Scott pulls back and shoots me a grin. "That's incredible, Noelle. Congratulations."

I smile, my arms dangling over his shoulders. "Whatever you said to him—"

"Nope." He kisses the side of my neck. "It's all you, baby. You gotta start taking credit for your hard work."

"He wants to take us to dinner when we're in New York next," I carry on.

Scott pauses again, his eyes searching mine. "I'd love to go."

I close my eyes and smile. "Thank you, Scotty."

I laugh as he lunges for me, tucking me underneath him as he lays us down on the couch. "It's all you, beautiful." He grasps the back of my thigh and hitches my leg up as he settles over me and kisses me. "It's always been all you."

I wrap my arms around his neck and pull him closer, tipping my chin up to deepen our kiss.

SCOTT and I play hooky for the day. We bundle up and step out into the freezing cold to build a snowman, to sled down the hill in his backyard, to embrace the delicious and wondrous feeling of giddy freedom. We revel in an afternoon of us, until our fingers are stiff with cold and our lips turn blue.

"I've got marshmallows," Scott says as I pour us mugs of hot chocolate.

He tosses me a package and I add a generous handful of mini marshmallows to each of our cups.

We sit at the kitchen island, thawing out, when he says, "I had a meeting the other night."

"Oh?" I blow on my hot chocolate.

"With the Huxley brothers. Out of Tennessee."

"They're part owners of the Tennessee Trojans," I comment, referring to the NBA team outside of Knoxville.

"Exactly. And…" He pauses, takes a long sip of his hot chocolate, and winks. "They're in."

"In?"

"For a Primrose Sweets pop-up shop. But the cupcakes have to be—"

"Trojan colors!" I exclaim, hopping off my barstool and barreling into him.

He laughs, catching me easily and wrapping me in his arms. "Or the Thunderbolts." He kisses the top of my head.

"I can't believe you did that. I mean, we weren't even talking a few days ago. I thought you couldn't stand me."

"Hey." He grips my arms and pulls away, fixing me with a look. "I'll never stop loving you, Noelle. You're it for me; whether you want me back or not is up to you. But I'll always be in your corner. Which is why…" He holds up one finger to indicate he needs a minute.

I falter back a step as he moves off the barstool and opens a kitchen drawer. He plucks out a sealed, manila envelope and slides it across the table to me.

"Happy New Year, Noelle DiSanto. I hope this next year is everything you want it to be." Scott hooks a hand into the pocket of his joggers and rocks back and forth on his feet, suddenly nervous.

I bite the corner of my lip, his nerves heightening mine. Slowly, I pick up the envelope and run my finger along the flap, loosening the adhesive. Then, I pull out the papers inside. As soon as I read the top line, I gasp, my hand flying up to cover my mouth. I glance at Scott, then the paper, then back up at Scott.

"You, this…" I shake my head, disbelief heavy in my tone. "You bought Primrose Sweets?"

He chuckles. "No." He moves next to me and points to the document on the kitchen island. "We bought the building. Well, you did." He taps to my name, indicating that the deed is in my name. And only my name. "No matter what happens, you'll always have a home for Primrose here in Boston. The building is yours, to expand and rent out as you wish."

I shake my head, still unable to process this. "You bought me a building?"

"I'm giving you a space of your own in a city, in a lifestyle, that seems to favor my career over yours. I know the hockey life wasn't your first choice. But, Noelle, I promise you, there is room in our relationship for both of our dreams to grow. Simultaneously. You're going to run an empire, beautiful girl. This is just one piece of the puzzle."

I rush him again, throwing my arms around his neck. This time, he lifts me up and holds me tightly. Then, he places me on the edge of the kitchen island and peers into my eyes. "Make a home with me, Noelle. Stay in Boston."

"Yes. I love you, Scotty."

He tugs me closer to the edge and runs his fingers along the column of my neck. "I hope you feel that way after spending New Year's with my family."

I laugh, hooking my legs around his waist. "I'll feel that way forever."

"Good." He cups my cheek, angling my face as he moves closer.

"And I intend to prove it," I whisper, just before our lips touch and I seal my promise with a kiss.

The thought makes me grin, just like when I was thirteen.

But Scott and me, we're locked up tight with an infinity of hugs and kisses.

EPILOGUE

SCOTT

Three Years Later

She's the most talented woman in the room. To me, she's the most talented woman ever.

I watch Noelle approach the bar, make effortless small talk that causes the bartender to chuckle. Her gown, a deep red, like her favorite pinot noir, ripples when she moves. She takes a sip of her wine, tipping her head toward the bartender and making one last quip that makes him smile.

Then she turns, her eyes find mine, and the love and light that shimmers in their depths reminds me what a lucky man I am to call her mine. She walks back to our table and my hand finds hers.

"Having fun yet?" She kisses my cheek.

"With you? Tonight? Always," I reply.

We both turn toward the stage as the MC for tonight's ceremony, an awards dinner, welcomes everyone. My thumb brushes over Noelle's diamond engagement ring and wedding band, tracing the smooth gold. I still can't believe this woman said yes to a life with me. We tied the knot nearly two years ago and our lives have been a chaotic, beautiful, exciting blend ever since.

While there have certainly been challenges with coordinating our schedules and making sure we spend the time together we need, we've also doubled down on each other's dreams, approaching the hockey world and baking industry with our collected efforts.

While I continue to manage a big part of the Hawks franchise, I promoted Jayde. She's heartily taken on the role of liaising with senior management, serving as a go-between, so I don't have to be at every meeting or on every call. I also handed off a lot of my business abroad in the hotel and restaurant sectors to trusted advisers, freeing up more time for Noelle and the launch of her dream.

More bakeries. More pop-up shops. With Primrose Sweets Philadelphia excelling and Primrose Sweets Chicago on deck, Noelle is starting to expand west. But it's been the pop-up shops that have really put her on the map. She's now in over twenty-five arenas around the country, putting her background in sports and her passion for baking, to excellent use. While it may not have been her original goal, I think she truly loves the pop-up shops that have become integral to her brand.

A brand that we're celebrating tonight.

"Please help me in welcoming to the stage, Scott Reland, owner of the Boston Hawks and husband to Noelle DiSanto Reland," the MC announces.

"Ready, beautiful?" I kiss Noelle's cheek.

She blushes as most of the eyes in the room swing toward us. She lets out a slow exhale and squeezes my hand once before releasing it.

I chuckle as I walk toward the podium, thrilled to be speaking at tonight's ceremony.

"Good evening, everyone," I address the crowd. "You know, over the past few years, I've had the privilege to attend several of these dinners. Some to speak at, others to celebrate the success of the Hawks. All of them have been special and rewarding and have filled me with so much gratitude for this community. But tonight's ceremony is by far my favorite.

"Because tonight, I have the immense pleasure of talking to you about my favorite person in the world: my wife." I pause to allow for the claps and cheers that ring out. When I catch Noelle's eye, I note the rosy glow that spreads across her cheeks and love that my words affect her.

"Noelle DiSanto Reland is a true visionary. Not many could have blended their intimate knowledge of the sports industry with a passion for baking, yet that's what Noelle has accomplished. Primrose Sweets is now in three cities in the Northeast and is expanding to the Midwest, with a Chicago location, later this year. But for cupcake lovers in other parts of the country, you can try the best cupcake you'll ever have, in your home team's colors, at twenty-five different pop-up stands in stadiums throughout the country." More clapping and cheers. I grin. "Tonight, we're here to honor and celebrate the woman who made all of this happen in just a handful of years. Noelle"—I stare right at her—"your dedication, perseverance, and passion is a joy to witness. I am so grateful to be your husband and to learn and grow by your side. It's *my honor* to present Boston Businesswoman of the Year to you. Congratulations, beautiful."

As Noelle makes her way to the stage, many in the audience stand and clap for her. She ascends the stairs slowly, making sure to clutch her dress. But God is she radiant, her eyes sparkling, her curls pulled away from her face.

I kiss her cheek and hand her the award. "Love you, baby."

"Love you more, Scotty," she murmurs back.

Then, she turns toward the crowd, and I step back to watch my wife shine.

"She's one hell of a woman," the MC says to me as Noelle begins her thank-you speech.

"I'm one lucky man," I respond, the words ringing true.

While I've heard the rumblings and snickers over the past two years that I'm whipped, that I stepped down from my career to support Noelle's, that Noelle calls the shots in our home, it never bothered me. Because I got exactly what I want.

A house filled with love, laughter, and warmth. A home brimming with family and friends for holiday meals. Christmas traditions, new and old. Early-morning coffees and late-night, after-dinner drinks, with a woman who makes my heart race. A few months ago, we started trying to conceive and I'm hopeful, excited, that in the next year, we may have our own baby news to announce.

But right now, I'm grateful to soak up this moment, celebrating the love of my life and the success we've found together. I'm thankful to be married to one hell of a woman. To be the luckiest guy I know.

I HOPE you loved Noelle and Scott's swoony, mature, and slightly forbidden romance in *The Score Keeper*! I've loved every moment spent with the Boston Hawks and these characters have taken up residence in my heart. So much so, I'm not ready to say good-bye to this world. Instead, I'm expanding it. I can't wait to introduce you to the Tennessee Thunderbolts!

IF YOU'RE desperate to know how Noah and Indy fare in Tennessee and what becomes of the new Thunderbolts, make sure you preorder Hot Shot's Mistake, a workplace, hockey romance, featuring recently traded New York Shark, Devon Hardt! It releases May 12 and you don't want to miss it!

OR, start the series from the beginning! Meet Noah and Indy in *The Sweet Talker*, now free!

THANK YOU!

The Boston Hawks Hockey Series has consumed my life for the past eighteen months and I wouldn't want it any other way. I've loved spending time with these incredibly swoony men and smart, go-getter women. Writing this series meant spending my days (and nights!) with a group of tight-knit friends. It wouldn't have been possible, or come together so quickly, without these wonderful women who have become my friends.

Amy Parsons, Becca Mysoor, Erica Russikoff - THANK YOU for all the time, energy, and advice you've given me. Your insights have strengthened the Hawks books and I'm grateful for all the encouragement whenever I hit a roadblock.

Melissa Panio-Peterson - I appreciate your commitment to the romance book world every day and I'm so grateful we've become friends!

Virginia Carey, Julia Heudorf, and Amber - Thank you for your eye to detail and for catching all the things (typos and plot holes included) that I miss.

THANK YOU!

Kate Farlow at Y'all. That Graphic - many thanks for creating a series of covers I adore. *The Score Keeper* cover captures Scott perfectly!

Dani Sanchez at Wildfire Marketing - working together is the absolute best! Thank you for all the calls, planning, and re-planning to help this series soar.

The wonderful women at Give Me Books Promotions — Thank you for all your support in sharing the word, and love, for the BHH books.

Bloggers, Bookstagrammers, and Booktok - Infinite thanks for your generous sharing of romance books. I truly appreciate every time you shout out a book you adore!

Readers - all my love for your continued support on this journey. Thanks for allowing me to live my dream. Thank you for cherishing this team as much as I do.

Home Team - I love you all the world. Always.

ALSO BY GINA AZZI

Knoxville Coyotes Football:

Faked and Fumbled

Surprised and Sacked

Trapped and Tackled

The Burnt Clovers Trilogy:

Rebellious Rockstar

Resentful Rockstar

Restless Rockstar

Tennessee Thunderbolts:

Hot Shot's Mistake

Brawler's Weakness

Rookie's Regret

Playboy's Reward

Hero's Risk

Bad Boy's Downfall

Lock 'Em Down

Boston Hawks Hockey:

The Sweet Talker

The Risk Taker

The Faker

The Rule Maker

The Defender

The Heart Chaser

The Trailblazer

The Hustler

The Score Keeper

Second Chance Chicago Series:

Broken Lies

Twisted Truths

Saving My Soul

Healing My Heart

The Kane Brothers Series:

Rescuing Broken (Jax's Story)

Recovering Beauty (Carter's Story)

Reclaiming Brave (Denver's Story)

My Christmas Wish

(A Kane Family Christmas

+ *One Last Chance* FREE prequel)

Finding Love in Scotland Series:

My Christmas Wish

(A Kane Family Christmas

+ *One Last Chance* FREE prequel)

One Last Chance (Daisy and Finn)

This Time Around (Aaron and Everly)

One Great Love

The College Pact Series:

The Last First Game (Lila's Story)

Kiss Me Goodnight in Rome (Mia's Story)

All the While (Maura's Story)

Me + You (Emma's Story)

Standalone

Corner of Ocean and Bay

www.ingramcontent.com/pod-product-compliance
Lightning Source LLC
Chambersburg PA
CBHW032221190726
48289CB00007BA/2336